The First of
Midnight

Marjorie Darke
Cover illustration by Jane Ray

BARN OWL BOOKS

BARN OWL BOOKS

157 Fortis Green Road, London, N10 3LX

First Published by Kestrel Books 1977
This edition Barn Owl Books, 2007
157 Fortis Green Road, London, N10 3LX

Distributed by Frances Lincoln,
4, Torriano Mews, Torriano Avenue, London, NW5 2RZ

A CIP catalogue record for this book is available from the British Library

ISBN (13 digit) 978 1 903015 64 3

Designed and typeset by Skandesign
Printed in the UK by Cox and Wyman

Introduction

Living in a multiracial city where Chinese, Polish, Jamaican, Irish, African, rubbed shoulders with people who at a glance would be taken to be from a long line of 'white'-British, I began to wonder what we mean when we say we are English. Do we have to be born in England I asked myself? Do our parents have to be born here . . . grandparents even? Did the colour of our skin have any bearing? And what of any cultural differences? The questions would not go away. They filled my mind. Somehow among all the growing fascination with the enigma, the threads of a story started to twist and multiply.

I began to read anything that might help sort these thoughts. Reading, thinking, pondering day after day, night after night, those threads began to weave together. I learned that the slave trade had been a source of wealth in this country certainly as far back as the seventeenth century, if not longer. The evil triangular shipping-run took most of the stolen Africans to work on plantations, but some did arrive and remain in England. Excitement grew as the story-idea developed. A slave would arrive in Bristol . . . somehow get away . . . settle perhaps . . . begin a family whose descendants could be traced to the present day . . .

It was all there waiting to be told. *But* one mountainous problem remained unresolved. How could a present-day middle-aged 'white' woman have the impudence to think she could truly see into the thoughts, upbringing and experiences of a young eighteenth century African man?

The problem seemed insurmountable until a book by James Pope-Hennessey called SINS OF THE FATHERS opened the door. An excellent book in its own right, but it was through the indexed list of bibliography at the back the I first came to meet OLOUDAH EQUIANO. This amazing eighteenth century African, stolen from his home in what was then known as the Gold Coast, was taken and sold into slavery in Barbados. He might have lived and died in obscurity if his master, a naval officer, had not had a kindly streak. Recognising the intelligence of this lad, he sent him to school when on land, and when on board ship allowed him to acquire the skills of navigation – something forbidden to slaves. He learned to speak and write in the English language. What was more in later years he wrote his autobiography! This treasure I was able to borrow from the British Library – a wonderful ancient leather bound book from which Olaudah seemed to reach out his hand to me, spanning the two hundred years between us. He told me about his upbringing, how the evil slave traders tore him from home and loving family at the age of twelve, the horrors of the slave ships – it was all there, a solid rock on which to build.

Several British ports grew fat on the back of this trade. I picked Bristol as the setting for my story because I know the city well, and it is rich in history. Slowly, over many days, nights, months, the eighteenth century people began to emerge out of the mists in my mind. They multiplied, some brutal, others kindly, and all talking in the Bristol way of the time – some of their words and phrases rightly considered unacceptable today. But being true to such language is vital when creating an atmosphere of authenticity, and makes the history come alive. The sights and sounds and smell of the place grew with these characters. Equalling the importance of my slave, who had been given the slave-name Midnight by his masters, another person emerged. Jess, a kitchen wench, as much a slave as Midnight, and in some ways more deprived, never having known any family. We meet her being sold off in a tavern. It is the last straw of dignity. She makes a run for freedom and at last, in a desperate bid to escape her pursuers, boards a ship at anchor in the quay, the ship where Midnight is captive . . .

Prologue

He would never forget his first taste of English fog. A wet white wall that ate through clothes, flesh and senses, letting him loose in a limbo world to face the evil English Spirits. Were they evil though? Yes . . . yes . . . anything that existed in these secret mists, shunning sun, warmth, life, could only be evil. They sucked all courage from your heart and all reasonable thoughts from your mind. No hate in them – that was too hot an emotion, but he could feel a cold malevolence. How could you appease such ghosts? At home there had always been a chance of soothing a ruffled Spirit with libations of wine or freshly killed chicken's blood. But what good was a libation to these bloodless wraiths? Nevertheless, he twice offered his rations of rum, pouring it over the side of the two-masted brig as they lay becalmed off the coast of Cornwall.

The second day Dando caught him at it.

'Hey . . . Midnight! That's good grog th'bist throwing overboard. Fog's got into th'brains.'

The fog had got into his brains.

'My brains, your brains, Captain's brains. We're in prison forever if . . .' He broke off short, remembering how many times he had been made to look a fool and worse.

'If what?' Dando asked.

Midnight remained stubbornly silent.

Dando grabbed his coat sleeves. 'Say summat can't thee?' and when there was still no answer: 'I'll tell Cap'n th's been stealing rum. Th'knows what that'll bring!'

He felt sick. A flogging? Strung up by the heels? Hot pitch on his back like poor Billy Waring?

Dando pulled him close - crabbed monkey face a paper's distance from the satin black skin – grinning and whispering: 'Which is it to be?'

'I pour offerings to the Spirits of the Fog,' Midnight said. 'That way we're released and can sail to safety up the Bristol Channel.'

Dando roared with laughter, slapping his shoulder. 'Th'should'st've been a parson by rights, Midnight. What with th'gentleman's speech and th'fancy for the other world. Here . . . Isaac! Heard what the nigger's been up to now?'

'What's that?' bellowed a voice without a body.

'Doin' his bloody witch-doctor turn. Pouring grog over the side.'

'I'll smash his bleedin' head in for un. Where is he?'

Midnight did not stir. If there was going to be a fight, he could hold his own. He said quietly to Dando: 'You have no god then . . . no devils . . . no ghosts . . . no superstitions? I remember that time in Jamaica when . . .'

'Shut th'gob or I'll shut it for thee,' Dando growled, backing off.

Midnight stared at him unblinking.

Dando said harshly: 'Why don't th'get back to th'bootlicking? That way Cap'n'll maybe hear thee out.'

'What's in your mind?'

Dando cackled. A shrivelled threatening sound. 'Time'll tell,' and he backed even further until the fog began to separate them.

Midnight continued to stare, knowing it was his only defence. Hiding the empty frightening hold that lived inside him. But Dando lingered, as if something physically restrained him . . . and out of the fog blanket came a single scream; thin, eerie, sexless. A silence – then another that faded and dulled.

'Holy Mother o'God! What was that?'. Dando breathed.

No further sound. Nothing. Even the faint creak and lap of ship and sea was suspended. Then the vessel came alive. Footsteps pounded up from the fo'c'sle. There were shouts and oaths as men stumbled over each other, unable to see more than a stretched hand in front of their noses. Dando melted into the fog, pulled by the noise, but Midnight went delicately towards the brig's starboard side and, with the rail to guide him, moved aft, in the direction of the Captain's quarters.

After the first paralysing sounds when he thought the Spirits had answered him, he had known the screams were human. His acute hearing had located the sounds and he was stealthily moving towards them. He skirted the dim shape that was the long boat, treading like a cat over the greasy deck. Every sense alert. Even so the meeting was unexpected. A sombre shape parted the fog. A man staggering under a dead weight. Midnight became still, blending with the dark wood, but he was too close. The body fell against his shoulder almost knocking him off balance. He saw the ugly stain on the dingy brocade waistcoat that spread out to the full shirt sleeve, and caught a brief glimpse of staring eyes in a white face. The mouth moved only slightly, and then the body slid over, lost to sight before it splashed down into the leaden sea.

But there was no escape from the pale expressionless eyes of the Captain. For a long moment he was netted by them, as the deck buzzed and throbbed with noise. At last he was released. The Captain turned, dissolving into the fog. A voice boomed:

'**MR CAREY** . . . bring some order on deck! All hands

below except those on watch.'

Separate in his veil of fog, Midnight felt the first stirring of wind against his cheek.

One

'Who'll bid for the wench?' Samson Orry gripped Jess round her narrow waist and swung her on to the tavern counter. 'Sharp as a tack, shipmates. Sharp nails an' all!' He rubbed a ham-like fist over four long scratches that disappeared into his wild black beard. Scratches made only a few minutes before.

Jess shivered, looking down at the upturned faces that stared at her with idle curiosity. Not a flicker of concern. Nobody cared if she lived or died. But that was the way of it as long as she could remember.

Samson scratched in the thick black hairs on his huge arms that were pitted by spark burns from the forge. 'Come, shipmates. An offer. Surely one of thee needs a drudge? As good a one as th'll find in all Bristol. She's skinny but tough. See!' He lifted the threadbare ratteen skirt, feeling her legs up to the knee. Jess kicked out, catching the handle of his tankard so that a puddle of porter slopped on to the counter.

'Careless slut!' Samson roared, giving her a stinging blow across the ear.

''Twas thee as made her do it, Sam.'

Jess looked through held tears at the blurred hunched shape who had spoken up for her. She blinked and the shape resolved into a broad stunted man with hands that almost touched his knees. His large untidy head was set close to shoulders which rubbed against the long lobes of his ears. He grinned, showing a row of black broken teeth. 'Here's to thee, gal. I likes spirit!' He took a mouthful of ale, some of it dribbling down into his stubble.

'Th'could do with a moll, Garty. Since thy old lady kicked the dust from her heels th've no soul to warm the bed.'

Garty grinned again. An evil grin, with no trace of warmth. 'A man can do without them comforts,' he said. ''Sides, I like more flesh on my women. But I'll give thee two shillings for the wench. I needs someone to cook and wash for me.'

'Two shilling, he says . . . what good's two shilling in these hard times?' Samson stretched out his arms, appealing to the crowd.

'It'ud do to buy us a few drinks with, Sam,' a woman called from the far end of the smoke-blackened room. Over the tops of the heads Jess stared at her, hunting for help that she knew would never come. 'I'd be kind to thee . . . see if I didn't!' The woman winked at Samson.

'We all know thy kindness, Betsy!' somebody called. 'Five minutes up Old Nick's Entry and th'pockets cleaned of every last farthing!'

There was a burst of laughter and the woman shrieked something that was lost in the hubbub. On her lonely perch, cut off from the amiable mindless warmth of the mob, Jess shifted, taking a cautious step back towards the edge of the counter. She had no plan of escape, only a desperate need not to be a spectacle. If she was cat slinky, she could slide below the counter. Take her chance on slipping out of the door into the street and away. No good looking further than that.

But even as the thought crowded her mind, the chance was gone. Samson grabbed her ankle. 'Thee ain't going nowhere, me gal.'

Jess pulled violently. The tears she'd mastered got the better of her. 'I ain't . . . thy slave!' she sobbed. 'Th'cant sell me.'

'Who paid five pound for thee seven year back?' Samson demanded.

'That were prentice money.'

'Call it what th'likes. The overseer at the Old Mind ain't going to argue. He got his money and was glad to see the back of thee. I ain't finding no wench for charity. I've me rights and thee b'long to me. Seven years' meals th'had o' me. Not to mention clothes. There's no one as'll disagree.'

Again Jess tried to wrench her ankle out of his grasp, but she had no more chance of freeing herself than a snared rabbit.

'Let go of me. What of my rights? I be free. I ain't one of them niggers to be sold like they used to at the Trow.' But it was no good. All she managed to do was lose her balance. Her legs shot up and Samson's tankard skidded across the counter, spilling the rest of the porter over the floor. Amid a roar of laughter and applause, she landed on her back.

'She's a regular little fighting cock!' 'I'll wager a pint o' the best on her to win!' 'Done!'

'Hellfire and brimstone!' Samson growled. 'I'll take th'two shilling, Garty. She's yourn! Look to th'self though, she's as spiteful as a witch's cat!'

'I can manage. Th'needn't worrit!' Garty fished in his pocket and brought out two coins. 'She'll do me fine.'

Jess – her blunt nose coming in contact with Samson's hand as she coiled round – bit him. Samson yowled, let go, and she was over the back of the counter crouching down, pushing and wriggling through stinking legs and skirts that reeked of an unwashed lifetime. Then began a game of cat and mouse. Legs opened and closed. Sometimes she got through. More often she didn't. The doorway was a smiling mouth that welcomed her. Almost she was there. Another shove and . . .

'Got thee, me lover!'

Jess felt herself being lifted high. She was passed from hand to hand. Pinched and squeezed. Faces leered, and all the struggling in the world was not a bit of use. She was firmly planted back where she started – on the wet counter.

'I know how to deal with thee, my wench,' Garty said. His overlong arms surrounded her and before she knew what was happening the strings of her skirt were untied. Garty pulled and Jess kicked him. The crowd cheered.

The stout landlord, who had been down in the cellar fetching a fresh keg of ale, lowered it to the floor. 'What's going on? Here, Garty . . . I'll not have th'stripping a wench in my tavern. This ain't no bawdy house. Leave her be! Samson, th'should see to her. She's yourn, ain't she?'

'I ain't,' Jess said, and kicked again. Her skirt dropped, leaving her standing in petticoat shreds.

The landlord took hold of Garty's collar. 'Get out!'

'I ain't going without my property,' Garty whined.

'Out!'

'The wench is his,' Samson said. 'He just took her off me hands.'

'Paid an' all,' Garty said, sidling crab-like towards Jess as well as he could, managing to stand on her skirt. 'She tried to run off. Stole some money from me pocket. Two shilling it were.'

'Shame, Garty Jenks! Th'gave un of thy own free will!' came a voice from further down the room.

The landlord could make no sense of it. He let go of Garty and shouted: 'They be waiting for the Battle this half

16

hour out in St Thomas's Street. Get to it, Samson. Th'bist the leader.'

'Another pint then, to mop up the dust and put strength in me arms,' Samson said. 'The wench knocked over me porter. Th'can charge this un to her!'

'How can I pay?' Jess demanded. 'I ain't got a brass farthing. Th'bist that mean.

'Th'can wash pots, can't thee?' Samson lifted his replenished tankard and poured the ale straight down his open throat. 'Forward the smiths! I'll wager the lot we'll slay them coopers and carpenters this year!'

There was a roar of approval from most of the mob. Someone called: 'Put th'money in th'muscles, Sam. Mine's on the coopers. They'll pulp thee!'

Samson's face mottled. He slammed down his tankard. 'Who said that? Th'wouldn't say as much to me face. Wait till I get at thee! Th'll be raw meat!'

'Save th'spleen for the Battle, Sam,' the landlord advised, and the crowd joined him, demanding action.

'Show un, Sam . . . in the street, Sam . . . mash un to pulp . . .' and the same lone voice: 'It'd be a sight better'n last Shrove Tuesday if th'managed that!' breaking into a chant of: 'Seventeen hundred and eighty seven, The year Sam Orry goes to Heaven!'

'Hell, th'mean.'

A bellow of laughter and a surge of bodies: squeezing and shoving round the door. Samson was amongst them, rooting after the unseen joker. Left behind, Garty Jenks swooped on Jess's skirt, and jerked. There was a ripping sound and she fell against the counter. He tucked the skirt under one arm.

'Just to make sure th'don't take off. When Battle's over I'll be back for thee.'

Jess snatched after her skirt, but he disappeared into the

crowd. Gradually the room emptied until the only people who remained besides herself, were the landlord and an old woman asleep on a stool by the far wall.

Jess eyed the landlord, sizing up the space between him and the door. But even if she'd been fully clothed the chance of escape was gone before it arrived. Without even glancing at her he said:

'Th'can stay with Granny here. And no monkey tricks! Her sleeps with one eye open. I'm off to watch the Battle. Mind . . . I'll not be more'n a stone's throw from the door, so rid th'self of thoughts about taking off. There's pots to wash and a broom under the counter. Busy th'self with that,' and he went out, closing the door.

Jess darted behind the counter. The broom was there, sawdust, a pile of dirty pots, two kegs of ale, but nothing that might do for a skirt. There was nothing in the room either. The only clothes were the greasy rags of the old woman. For the second time tears scalded her eyes. Tears of rage and frustration. Well, they weren't going to win this time. She'd find something or die. And she'd do it sharpish while the Battle kept everyone busy. That way there'd be less chance of getting caught. She mustn't be caught. There'd be a flogging or worse if they took her with stolen clothes. The trap door was under her feet, but what good was that? Nobody kept clothes in the cellar. She'd have to risk going through the door . . . have to! With a bit of luck the passage would be empty. The stairs were there. Steep and dark. Leading to mystery.

Jess swallowed, feeling her heart pump and thud. She crept to the door. Put her hand to the latch. Lifted. Across the room the old woman stirred and mumbled. ̶s became a statue, but it was all right. The latch clicked and the door opened. The door at the end of the ̶ge was open too, and framed in the light she could see the landlord's square back and bursting breeches. The roars and cheers of the crowd covered any sound she made and, like a wraith, she made for the stairs, sweating even in the bleak February cold at the thought of who she might meet in the unknown upstairs. But again it was alright. She opened the door at the head of the stairs and walked boldly in. If there was nobody it didn't matter, and if there was somebody, careful creeping wasn't going to make a ha'porth of difference.

There was a four-poster bed with tattered red hangings taking up nearly all of the floor space. The only other furniture was an old chest under the squat window. On it was one shoe with the buckle missing and a half-filled chamber pot. There was also a cracked and speckled mirror. Jess placed the lot on the floor and opened the chest.

Glory oh glory, breeches and a waistcoat! Nobody would be looking for a runaway lad. Quickly she pulled on the breeches. They were much too wide and fell down over her hips, so she tore off a strip of petticoat to tie round her middle, tucking the other rag ribbons inside for warmth. The waistcoat hung off her shoulders, but would have to do. She shut the lid of the chest and put back the pot, shoe and mirror, stopping for a moment to gaze at her reflection. An urchin stared back, neither male nor female. Stick legs in dirty grey stockings protruded from where the breeches finished and the cracked shoes were a woman's shape. Her mass of frizzy black hair was a woman's as well. With sudden inspiration she tore off another rag of petticoat and tied it back. She smiled in triumph, making her wide-set green eyes squeeze back into their thick black fringe of lashes. As a last touch she spat on the sleeve of Samson's cast-off shirt and rubbed the tear streaks from her thin cheeks. Then smartly saluted herself.

'Here's to thee, shipmate!' she said in a mock bass voice, giggled . . . and felt her skin shrivel. Unmistakably someone was coming up the stairs. There was nowhere but under the bed. She pushed into the dust, banging her head on the wooden underside. The door opened. A woman's voice called:

'That thee, Sal?'

From under the valance, Jess could see a pair of patched green shoes lapped by grimy skirt edges.

'Lordy!' said the voice. 'Left the slops an' all. She'll have to go. I ain't paying the slut for nothing. Just th'wait, my gal. There's a hiding for thee when th'gets back from th'gallivanting!'

The skirts twisted and swung, stirring dust which rose into Jess's nostrils. She hung on to the end of her nose, desperately killing the sneeze, but it refused to die. As the door shut, the sneeze burst out. To Jess it sounded like the end of the world.

The feet, which had started down the stairs, came back. The door opened and the valance flicked up. Brown eyes stared upside-down into green. A lined mouth stretched back in a screech. Jess didn't wait. Backing from under the bed, she made a dash for the door, twisting and ducking to avoid the out-stretched hand of the landlord's wife. Down the stairs she went, fast and flexible as a cat, followed by shrieks of: 'Come back th'little bastard . . .'

There was no point in stealth now. Surprise was everything. Surprise, speed and the blessed seething mob outside.

The landlord, partially blinded as he turned from sunlight into gloom, was aware only of a shadow; a stirring of air; a faint dull patter mixing into the rowdy mob-noise, and something brushing featherlight against his thigh as he waddled down the passage. He heaved his bulk around, but saw only the tightly wedged backs of the mob out in the street.

Jess wormed through the crush, at last emerging into daylight. In front the narrow street boiled with a confusion of heaving thrusting sweating bodies; behind, the crowd moved as the battling men staggered and shifted. It was almost impossible to know which were coopers and carpenters and which smiths. All struck out at random – a muddle of punching fists and kicking boots. Next to her a fat woman with bulging eyes and arms like balloons, yelled:

'Whack the taters off un, Fred . . . go on give un a basting . . .'

The crowd caught up the shout and Jess felt excitement run through her. Drawn into the shouting clamour she would have forgotten her own danger if the Battle hadn't taken a sudden change of fortune. From somewhere out of the back ranks of the fighters, Samson rose up, towering head and shoulders over the rest of the mob. His face was purpling down the left side and one eye was closed. He bellowed something which Jess couldn't catch, but she knew his rage was at a peak. Nobody could stand against such fury. She felt her bones weaken in fear, though now his anger was not directed against her. He didn't even know she was there, but it seemed wiser to hide. She looked for an escape gap, but the crowd had shifted again and closed up. In alarm, she glanced back at Samson and saw him hit out wildly, lose his balance and crash back, knocking down the men behind like a row of ninepins. A cheer broke out. The coopers and carpenters surged forward. Without Samson's monumental strength, the smiths seemed to lose ground. But it wasn't the end. From a group of watching men on the opposite side of the road came a rallying cry:

'Come on lads . . . two agin one ain't fair. Let's give un a hand!'

They were the weavers followed by a few tottering sailors who had just come out of another tavern. As they passed Jess, flinging themselves into the Battle, she saw Garty Jenks among them. He hadn't seen her, but the closeness of him moved her to flight. She butted back into the crowd, straining through until she was free. Then ran and slipped and ran again, past the church, between the dignified houses on the new Bristol Bridge, dodging the tollkeepers who marvelled at her speed, and over to the Welsh Back where horse-drawn sleds wove between towers of kegs, hanks of rope, sprawling sacks and the beached masts of ships, and where she knew she could shrink unnoticed into a warren of warehouses, entries and cellars.

She found a dark crevice up an entry leading to a court, and crouched down, head on knees. There was a pain like a red-hot brand in her chest and her stomach groaned with hunger. No food since morning and then only a taste of beer and some burnt gruel. Samson had clouted her for it – the beginning of a long bad day. But she didn't want to think of what was gone. It was now that mattered. Now and tomorrow. Anything else was too big to handle. She was sure only of one thing. Nothing and nobody was going to make her slave for Garty Jenks, not even Samson. She'd slaved for him for the last seven year, and before that ever since she was born – eight or nine year was it – at the Old Mint? Difficult to hold fast to time. However long she had been there, the whole stretch was a dingy aching trail of work and beatings.

She tightened her hold on her knees, jabbing her nose further into the folds of her breeches and grimly tried to focus on what was to come. But thinking was difficult and planning impossible.   She sobbed dryly, fighting off real tears. The late afternoon slid into night, bringing a touch of frost and sapping the last of warmth and cheerfulness. Huddling away from the draughts, she tried to keep up her spirits by thinking of all the hated things she had left behind – the sweeping and scrubbing and lugging coals; Will's taunts and Samson's beatings; the damp bed of straw and sacks in the old scullery; worst of all, the threat of being passed on to Garty Jenks. But the gloom didn't lift, so she tried to make a triumph of running away, but even that had lost its glory. Worn out by hunger and fatigue, she slipped in and out of an uneasy doze as the night darkened.

Two

Jess was prodded awake by the toe of somebody's shoe. The somebody bent down, peering at her in the gloomy first light. She smelled bilious breath and heard a voice mumbling:

'What've we got? A bleedin' varmint in me place. Out th'goes! There's not so many warm spots as I can spare this'n.' The toe dug painfully into Jess's thin ribs.

She was so cold . . . fixed and frozen never to move again.

'Come on, th'varmint. Off with thee!'

Jess opened her eyes grudgingly. A shapeless bundle of dirty rags was in front of her, the face no more than a grey shadow. No one of consequence. If she had wanted to stay she'd have made a song and dance, but it was better to move. That way she might warm up. She stretched creakily. The toe jabbed.

'All right, th'old baggage. No need to kick. I'm off!' She got up and almost fell, stumbling on numbed legs into the alley. With her mind muzzy from sleep and cold, instinct alone turned her away from the Welsh Back, stretching out the distance between herself, the Old Market where Samson had his smithy, and all of yesterday. To add to her miserable state a bleak wind had got up, bringing with it a sweet tangy yeast smell that made her stomach roll and cry out. She'd have to get something inside her before much longer – even a swig of beer would be better than nothing. But it was far too early for any taverns or coffee houses to be open. Not that time made any difference when there was no money. If she was honest, no money meant no food – which left her with very little choice.

She followed her nose, turning into a passage which led to the back of a small bakery. The door was ajar, letting out the warmth and scent of heaven. Inside, under flickering rushlight, on a long wooden table scrubbed to whiteness, were the first trays of crusty bread.   The baker, with his back to her, was shovelling more loaves from the brick oven. Jess was in and out with the speed and turn of a ferret.   Clutching the hot loaf to her chest she fled, expecting every minute to hear shouts of: 'Thief . . . thief . . .' as she threaded between the wharves, arriving at a narrow lane not far from Marsh Street where the press gangs roamed. No one was about. Nevertheless uncertain fear kept her running.

The Frome was in smelling distance now and through a gap between overhanging houses she caught a glimpse of tall upright masts and rigging. Her senses sharpened. The sight and smell of the waterfront drew her as always, giving her enough courage to slip across to Broad Quay. Gabled houses fringed one side of the quay; on the other the river was thick with ships, brigs, schooners – cutting into the heart of the city. The quay turned steadily, the river with it, and on the hill beyond, church and rich houses floated ghostly in misty trees lit by an early yellow dawn. Jess didn't notice. All her attention was on her first bite of bread which tasted as if it had come straight from Paradise.

The moment didn't last. Further up the quay she saw movement. Two men – one rolling a keg. If she didn't find a safe corner to rest and eat she stood the chance of being caught. Then it would be Bridewell at least, if they didn't stretch her neck on the gallows. But where . . . where?

The men disappeared behind a distant quayside shed, but she dared not trust to luck and hid behind a winch. On the river the vessels creaked and groaned as a gust of wind caught them. It blew under her waistcoat as well, cooling her body where the hot loaf had been, making her shiver. Only one good thing to come of such cold – it kept the bugs from biting. She scratched, the itch coming with the thought, and looked across at a brig that was still low on the incoming tide. The deck was empty and silent. There were no lights – no sign of life. No one, not even a baker hunting for a thief, would think of looking there. She measured the mooring rope which stretched tight between bollard and brig. It was the ideal place!

Tucking the loaf into her shirt top, Jess wrapped herself monkey-like, legs and arms round the rope, swinging across the scummy water hand over hand, gripping and letting go with easy rhythm until she reached the side of the brig. She hung for a moment, listening for any hint of life. But there was nothing, and with a quick twist of her body she hoisted herself over the wooden rail to slither down on to the deserted deck.

Relief at having succeeded without being seen, quickly gave way to uneasiness. It was the first time she'd ever been on board ship. She'd never so much as set foot in a rowing boat! There was something creepy about the noises of water and wood that on shore were exciting. The fact that the brig rocked slightly under her feet, gave the impression it was still alive, like a great animal crouched ready to spring. She knew it wasn't so, but the feeling was so strong and strange, she crept into a space between one of the big masts and an open water butt, making herself small as she nibbled the bread, but too alert and wary to really enjoy the eating. Gradually the feeling lessened and she crawled out on to the open deck, peering about, and when nothing happened, grew confident enough to begin to explore. Rope was everywhere – rope and a curious sour vinegar smell. She stared up at the rigging that fretted against a sky of pearl. It would be easy to climb; easier than the single rope that had got her here. A broad rope ladder to take her above the mainmast to that platform – she would be able to see all Bristol. Dare she do it? The sailors swarmed like ants over the rigging . . . she'd seen them many a time. Dare she? Quickly up and back . . .

The teasing excitement of the idea disappeared in a burst of alarm. Behind her, the sound of footsteps climbing an unseen stairway. She raced for the protection of mast and water butt, caught the toe of her shoe on a raised nail and went sprawling. A head-on collision with a pair of black salt-stained leather boots. The boots staggered sideways with the impact, but the man inside them didn't fall.

'Hell's mouth!' It was a curious voice, light but clear with a slight rasping edge to it. Even in her panic as she scrabbled to rescue the half-eaten loaf, Jess noticed its individuality. A voice she wouldn't forget. She didn't dare look up and shrank into a ball, knees to chin, loaf held between crossed arms and her chest.

One of the boots poked at her. 'What the devil . . .'

Jess uncurled slightly and hooked an arm round the leg, hugging it to her side, scarcely enough breath left in her to do more than murmur:

'God save me . . . I didn't mean no harm,' tightening her grip with as much fervour as she held the loaf.

She was roughly shaken, but clung on until the man said:

'Leave go! Leave go or you'll send us both below to crack our skulls. Will you leave go, lad, and stand up . . .

UP!' With the command, he grasped Jess's arm and hauled her to her feet, then shook her like a piece of crumpled linen, both of them swaying on the edge of the hatchway. 'Now then – speak up!'

He pulled her with him to a more secure place, but there wasn't a chance of speaking even if she'd had breath or invention. The wedge of light lying on the open stairway leading down from the hatch fanned out and a voice draped in icicles called:

'Mr Lambert – there's a damned lot of noise on deck.' Stair treads creaked.

Jess froze where she was, keeping her eyes on the ground. The voice continued: 'And what is that?'

A tiny piece of resentment returned a wisp of courage to Jess. She raised her eyes to midriff level but no further. Two pairs of boots now. Two sets of breeches and the skirts of two full-bottomed coats. But where the newcomer was all black and chunky, her captor was a grey and cherry scarecrow. He spoke up for her.

'A lad with sea fever, it would seem, Captain Meredith.' There was humour in the voice and Jess sneaked a look. The face was lean and weather-beaten. Blue eyes set rather too close for handsomeness, and a loose full mouth that was half smiling, one corner higher than the other. He wore no hat or wig and his thick untidy hay-coloured hair was tied away from his face.

Her glance slid from this face to the other and she found herself observed by pale eyes set in bloated white flesh. The overall impression was of whiteness – skin, eyes, old-fashioned wig, square hands – emphasised by the severe blackness of the clothes. Gold lace trimming on the tricorn hat was the only relief. The eyes blinked once, slowly, like the passing of an inner skin over the eyes of a hawk. She found their contact unpleasant, but somehow couldn't pull her own away. The spell was only broken when the Captain looked over her head, saying:

'Drop him overboard. A rat back to the sewer.'

Jess took a step backwards, muttering under breath: 'God protect me and forgive me sins I didn't mean no wrong . . .' without believing in much except bruises, hunger and Fate which had a nasty way of turning the tables against her, but willing at the same time to try anything once.

'I'm not God, but I'll put in a word for you,' Mr Lambert said quietly, pushing her behind him. 'I'll take him along with me when I go on shore, sir. He seems harmless.'

'Harmless? A sewer rat. Diseased and verminous. Such pests must be exterminated.'

'Oh I doubt he's that bad, sir. Wiry for sure, but well fitted together and agile enough, I'd say.;

'You seem set on protecting him. What is he to you?' The Captain turned his hooded eyes full on Mr Lambert who hesitated and then said awkwardly:

'Nothing, save I'd give him a chance. Everyone should have a second chance.'

There was a brief silence. Each man seeming to be weighing some hidden sword. The captain suddenly turned his attention to Jess.

'Sea fever, is it?' he said. 'Snared a rat, have we? But even rats can learn. What have you got, rat? A loaf? Stolen of course. Rats always pilfer . . . their nature. We could dispense some justice and hang him from the bowsprit to save the courts the trouble. Take it from him, Mr Lambert.'

Jess opened her eyes wide, hugging the loaf to her. 'No,' she muttered, spitting crumbs. 'No!'

'Mr Lambert – the loaf!' ordered the Captain as if she

hadn't spoken.'

Mr Lambert licked his lips. 'The lad seems to be hungry,' he said cautiously, as if testing unknown ground.

Again silence; an arctic frosting of the air that had nothing to do with the weather.

'The loaf, Mr Lambert,' repeated the Captain, deadly quiet.

Jess saw the colour mount in the lean face, heard him say: 'He's a right to it sir. How do we know it's stolen?' and warmed to him, grateful he was willing to defend her, though fearful in case she was asked direct.

'Rights? Who are you to speak of rights?' The Captain's white face had greyed, his small mouth tightening into a cruel line. He went on: 'I'll remind you of your obligations. If you choose to disobey, it will be the worse for you.'

Mr Lambert took a deep breath and closed his eyes for strength. 'Sir, we are no longer at sea. Our discussion was closed ten minutes ago. The voyage is over; the hands paid off. We're about to part company.' .

'You are still on board.'

'But going, sir . . . going.'

'To prison I presume.'

Watching first one and then the other, Jess saw Mr Lambert flinch. She waited for his answer and when he remained silent, wondered what he must have done. The threat, if it was a threat, had taken all his nerve, and the seed of liking for him died within her. She knew she'd been right not to trust him, guessed she had lost his support and did the only thing possible – tore at the bread with her teeth, one bite, two . . . three – stuffing her mouth till the bread protruded and she could hardly chew. The last thing in the world she might have expected was to hear the Captain laugh. There was no joy in the sound, no warmth, no lightheartedness. When it ceased, he said: 'It would seem you are a born loser, Mr Lambert. Your chances gone with half the loaf, while my new cabin boy is revived and the heartier for it.'

Jess almost choked. *Cabin boy?* Forgetting her doubts she looked at her protector, but her wordless appeal was lost on him. He was restlessly scanning the quay, searching backwards and forwards.

'Set out the gangplank, Mr Lambert. It's no protection now. The lad will stay with me. Hands are not so easy come by for a slaver. He shall slake his sea fever to the full. You still hesitate? A conscience for his rights, I see. Let me put your mind at rest. Here is a shilling. My shilling is as good as the King's. No more and no less than any man takes for service with the fleet. You may take it on his behalf. He won't be needing it. Buy a few tankards of ale . . . or better still, buy yourself a place at the card table.' The sneer was so obvious, Jess wondered Mr Lambert didn't hit out. But he was too fearful, she could see that and despised him just a little.

The Captain had taken a small leather pouch from an inner pocket, pulled open the drawstring, extracted a shilling and was holding it out. The coin went from hand to reluctant hand. Jess could have wept. For the second time in two days she had been bought and sold. But it was no more than she should have expected. The only card she held was her disguise. No one had guessed she was anything but a boy. At least she wouldn't be made the doxy of this fearful black and white slug. Even the thought of such a thing made her shudder. Samson for all his ill-treatment and slave-driving had never tried to fondle her. Of the very few things that were her own, her chastity mattered most. She'd give that up when she pleased or she'd die an old maid. No one should tumble her in an alley . . . nor in this Godforsaken brig. She wouldn't let herself be used like the waterfront women – not now . . . not ever!

The sale was over. Mr Lambert sought her eyes, but she refused to meet them. He went to the starboard side of the boat and took hold of a broad plank, heaving at it while the Captain remained still and silent, watching. Jess stood paralysed, despair mounting inside, seeing the plank sliding into position. The man picked up a small portmanteau that had been hidden in shadow by the rail, and with one last sweeping look across the quay, climbed on to the gangplank. The last Jess saw of him was his gaunt back with the coat skirts swinging as he disappeared down towards the quay.

The Captain moved deliberately between her and the frail hope of escape. Jerking the loaf from her hands he shouted: 'Midnight . . . MIDNIGHT!'

Jess stared at him in terror, bewildered, hardly realising the extent of her changed situation. No longer on land. A thousand miles from Bristol for all the chance she had of getting away. And even if she could escape, what was there to go to? She had nothing; was nothing. No, that wasn't true – she had herself. She wouldn't cower. As she straightened her shoulders, the Captain roared again: 'Midnight, you evil rogue . . . show yourself!'

There was a scuffle and the sound of someone running across the deck. Jess turned sharply and saw a tall Negro coming from behind the mainmast. He was dressed neatly enough in grey breeches, white shirt and an ill-fitting blue coat, but was barefoot. His hair was black like her own, but curled tight against his head emphasising his broad cheekbones. Large dark eyes looked at her without any expression and all he said was: 'Sir?' in a voice both deep and guarded.

But the thing that caught and held her attention was the metal collar banding his neck. There were engraved letters on it which she could not read, because she had never learned.

'Where've you been hiding? Lazy idle vagabond!' The Captain leaned forward slapping him twice, fore and backhand, across the face.

The Negro took the blows without any change in his blank withdrawn look. 'The cuffs, damn you,' said the Captain. 'From my cabin. You know the box.'

Without a word the Negro turned and Jess saw the padlock fastening the collar at the nape of his neck. He went lightly down the hatchway and was gone, reappearing in a moment holding a shackling chain on either end of which was a clumsy iron ring, hinged and padlocked. Taking them, the Captain locked one on the Negro's left wrist, then grabbing Jess's right arm, fastened the other on her. He grunted, satisfied.

'You can guard each other,' he said, picking up the loaf again. 'Take the rate to the fo'c'sle, Midnight. He should feel at home there. And take care neither of you stir till I call.' Stunned, Jess remained where she was, understanding nothing.

Midnight tugged with his fettered arm: 'Come I show you.' She had no choice but to follow.

Three

'What's to become of me?' Jess ventured to ask.

They were sitting on two upturned kegs in the dark of the fo'c'sle – had been sitting for ever and longer, she felt. A square of light coming through the open hatch made half-hearted patterns through the ladder and silhouetted the Negro. He didn't answer and Jess felt uneasy, but having started to talk was determined not to be ignored. Perhaps he hadn't understood her?

'What'll the Captain do with me? How long do us have to stay here?'

Midnight shrugged. 'We stay until it is his pleasure that we go.'

Jess was startled, not by the idea, but by the way it was expressed. He sounded almost like the gentlemen who brought their horses to be shod at Samson's smithy, except for a slight foreign way of leaning on the wrong part of the words. It was not the speech of a deckhand. She'd heard enough of them cussing and blinding.

'Thee his servant?' she asked.

'Slave,' he corrected.

She looked at the polished coppery band, so different from the collars Samson forged along with fetters and thumbscrews for the slave trade. They were rough spiked things. 'Never seen a slave band like that afore.' He seemed uninterested, so she tried asking: 'Where do th'come from?'

'Here.'

'I mean afore that?'

'Jamaica.'

'And the Guinea Coast afore that?' she prompted, hoping for tales about unknown Africa that seemed to her as strange as the moon and as far away.

But he wouldn't answer and only shifted, rattling the chain.

'I've seen 'em loading up the Guineamen ready to sail for Africa,' she said, thrusting away the indignity of being shackled, cheering herself with talk. 'They take all sorts of fancy things to trade – brass basins, beads, looking glasses . . . last time I saw great bales of cotton stuff, all red and blue and gold. Like sunsets they were . . . lovely!' She sighed, coveting the memory, then went on: 'Did the Cap'n buy thee from the Guinea Coast and ship thee across the sea?' She was determined to get an answer.

But his reply was a list of questions: 'What of you? Your name, your trade, your place of living?'

She stiffened, suspecting that he was making fun of her. She wasn't going to stand for that! 'Th'tongue's too long,' she said. ''Twas me as asked the question.'

'Questions,' he said. 'And too many.'

Well! If that was the way of it, she'd not say another word . . . no, not one!

They sat in silence, listening to the wind whistling through cracks and crannies between the planks of the old brig. The cold was like weasels biting and the strong strange musky smell of the fo'c'sle played on her stomach that was already protesting over the gobbled bread. She hadn't intended speaking again, but curiosity nagged her – besides, talking would keep her mind off her queasy innards.

'Is this a slaver then? How many folks did it carry?' and

when he refused to answer, added stiffly: 'Jess . . . that's what I'm called,' as a first move to soften him - and then remembered she was supposed to be a boy.

Oh Christmas! But a nigger wouldn't know one name from another, would he? Anyway 'Jess' was near enough right for boy or girl.

There was no response, so she went on hastily: 'The Cap'n called thee Midnight. Is that all of th'name?'

'No.'

There was another long pause.

'Well go on then, tell us the rest of it.'

'Why should I tell you anything?'

'I was only asking kindly like,' Jess said, nettled. 'Besides, th'know mine now, and I'll tell thee my trade like thee asked. 'Tis that of a smith.' It was near enough true. Hadn't she cleaned and swept for Samson long enough? She'd watched him working, learned the feel and way of shaping iron through eyes and ears and nose. She only lacked strength, that was all. Not that a girl would ever be allowed to touch the great hammers or take the white-hot metal from the furnace with the giant tongs. There was nothing for girls, only drudgery and breeding, specially paupers like herself.

Midnight had turned his head. His face was in darkness, but he must be looking at her. She looked down, afraid that the shirt and waistcoat had shaped themselves around her small breasts and so betrayed her.

'As for any home, I've none, nor did I ever have,' she said quickly to distract him from too much thinking. 'So now th'knows all, and owes me summat in return.'

He laughed then, and she was surprised. It was the first friendly sound that day; real and infectious. She found herself smiling.

'Perhaps I'll tell you one day, if we chance to get

acquainted, but for the present my name is all I have that belongs to me alone,' he said.

Jess felt cheated. The warmth that had come with his laughter faded, and she felt he had tricked her into saying more than she intended. Absurdly, she felt hurt; the more so because she understood his feelings about his name. Sympathy and resentment jostled each other. The chain joining the handcuffs chinked and pulled at her wrists as he moved, and resentment won. To be chained like a common criminal and to a nigger – oh it was too much! Her earlier fears about what terrors lay in store returned, all the more powerful because for a few minutes she had forgotten them. But she wasn't going to show she was scared. Her mouth tightened. She would be silent as the grave this time – give her mind to getting free.

But there was no time to rub two thoughts together before the square of light was partially blotted out by the Captain's bulk. His harsh voiced shouted at them as if they were at the top of the rigging, rather than a stone's throw from his feet.

'Up on deck. Like sparks or I'll have the hide off you.'

Midnight was up and moving before Jess had time to collect her wits. She was obliged to follow, stumbling after him as he took the ladder two at a time.

'Any property of mine must look respectable on shore.' Captain Meredith held out a pair of white worsted stockings and some cracked leather shoes with tarnished buckles to Midnight. 'I have my estate to consider . . . my kingdom!' He surveyed Jess, then extended one hand and took her shirt between finger and thumb. His expression of disgust made her bristle.

'I ain't got the pox,' she said tartly.

His answer was a stinging blow across her face and the curt words: 'You stink. I'll not have my servants smelling like a cesspit, but there's naught to be done for the present.'

Jess put her hand to her burning cheek, anger overcoming her terror, muttering: 'I ain't no servant to thee.'

The Captain wiped his fingers on Midnight's coat. 'A cabin boy on board and a servant on shore, or prisoner in Newgate. Those are your prospects. Take your pick.' Under his snake-like gaze she became dumb; anger turning to fear.

All the time Midnight was silently pulling on his white stockings and buckling his shoes. Now he straightened up, but continued to act as if she didn't exist, though she'd been forced to move as he moved. It was humiliating.

The Captain walked to the head of the gangplank and paused for a moment, stroking the worn rail with an almost loving touch.

'Au revoir, my princess,' he murmured. 'One kingdom for another, but I shan't forget nor abandon you.' Then without another word he pointed to a small metal-bound box and a canvas bag standing side by side, and climbed from the brig to the plank to the quay below.

There was nothing for it but to go with him. Even if she hadn't been linked to the blackamoor, the cards were stacked against flight. Too many people had an interest in her whereabouts and she didn't have much faith in her disguise. Apart from that, life had taught her to pry because sometimes doing so turned up the most surprising things. Like the time she'd found Will Pegg's pockets full of iron nails he'd filched from Samson. She'd taxed him with trading them for snuff, which was his passion, and he'd not denied it. That bit of knowledge had kept him sweet for weeks. He'd given her a few sugar pieces, which she'd taken, and even offered several pinches of snuff, which she hadn't.

It was easy to hope that good might come out of this plaguy mess, but at least it was different from anything that had happened to her before. Hope fed her nosiness and kept her plodding beside Midnight, who'd had an awkward job swinging the box on to his shoulder. The canvas bag she was carrying was awkward too and banged against her legs, threatening to trip her up. A few people were staring. They must look like something from a fair booth – a shrimp and a black giant tied together! She was glad to reach the door of the Seven Stars where she could rest the bag, though she was screwed up with fear that Garty might pop out of some alley, or Samson erupt like a volcano from the bowels of the tavern.

'A room for myself and some corner to house my two servants,' Captain Meredith said, walking inside. 'Come on – let's see sparks!'

'Thompson at your service,' said the landlord coming to meet them with a welcoming smile which disappeared quickly as he saw Midnight – his glance sliding from the metal collar to the handcuffs and on to Jess's flushed face. She felt another flare of alarm.

'Th'servants did th'say, sir?' he asked.

Captain Meredith treated him to one of his freezing looks. 'Yes. You do hear – and I do not repeat.'

The landlord coughed, sniffed and rubbed his chin. 'Hand-bolted?' There was a suggestion of disapproval.

'I use my servants my way. If they behave in a manner that deserves punishment, they are punished. No one interferes.'

'Of course . . . of course. But it is more than that. 'Tis the collar, sir. Don't th'know as it's against the law to hold a slave in England now?'

'Where I go Meredith law goes,' the Captain said

loudly. 'A room – you're being too slow.'

'I'll provide the cleanest with the best service in all Bristol. Good victuals and ale to any man but a slave master. All men be free. I stand by that.'

Watching, Jess thought the Captain would do murder. His white face took on a curious mauve tinge and the loose flaps of skin under his cheeks quivered.   'Waterfront scum!' There was enough venom in his voice to poison the landlord who managed to remain unmoved.

'Thompson's law stands here, sir, and I'll bid you good day,' he said with hard-won civility.

The two men measured each other. Size for size they were equal, and all the Captain's air of authority and frosty hypnotic stare was met by dogged resistance. The Captain lurched forward, his arms stiff by his sides.

'You have risked everything. I'll stamp on you. You are done!'

'Good day, sir,' repeated the landlord.

Captain Meredith trembled on the edge of violence, then whirled around shouting: 'Midnight, you ugly devil, get that box back on your shoulder and take your lazy body out of this place. You too,' cuffing Jess. 'I have business at the Llandogger Trow that can't wait on playacting.'

Four

Early dinner had been laid in a private upstairs room at the Trow. A great honey-baked ham crusted with cloves sat on a pewter serving dish on a side table, along with a roasted green goose, a pig's face, boiled tongue, a dish of oyster sauce, another of cheesecake and a tower of damson cheese. There were also jugs of ale, bottles of amber wine, port and Bristol 'milk' – the finest sherry in all England.

Jess was overcome, but not with joy. Saliva poured into her mouth and her stomach groaned. From the corner where she squatted on a stool, she watched Midnight quietly serving the six people sitting at the long table in the centre of the room and, in spite of her hunger, was impressed by the careful, unobtrusive way he worked – standing always on the left of each person, never knocking against them or even brushing the backs of their tall chairs. She decided he was a good deal more accomplished than the people he served. One in particular, the only woman present, was a most untidy eater – dropping meat from her fork and slopping sauce down her tight laced bodice that showed between the lapels of an odd mannish jacket of brown allepeen. But it wasn't just her eating habits that kept Jess's eyes rivetted, or her extraordinary white wig that rose to a height of two feet or more and was decorated with bunches of false cherries and violets – it was the way she conducted herself. She laughed often; a great sudden masculine sound, jerking her arms as if elbowing the air out of the way. Her brightly rouged cheeks crinkling into a fine network of wrinkles as she showed large yellow teeth.

'You'll be the death of me, Mr Loveitt, dammee if you won't,' she said, her voice as loud as her laugh.

The wizened man in black addressed as 'Mr Loveitt' said precisely:

'It was no joke I assure you, Miss Jarman. It would seem the voyage hardly warrants the payment of this dinner.' He bit delicately into a strip of goose breast.

Miss Jarman's smile died. She looked down the table to Captain Meredith facing her. 'That so, Captain?'

He nodded, suitably solemn. Round the table the faces expressed dismay, disbelief, doubt. Jess, watching Midnight, saw him glance swiftly from one to another, his look cold, even scornful.

A stout man in sober grey that contrasted with his many-coloured face and cheerful manner, leaned towards the Captain. 'I'd heard rumours, but discounted them. So it's true that the cargo was poor.'

'Not at the start, Doctor, let me be clear on that point. As fine a herd of slaves as you could wish – one hundred and twenty prime males and another seventy young females, half a dozen or so children and two suckling babes. Before we'd sailed out from Calabar more than a day, three more were born. Died there too.'

'And the rest?' asked the Doctor.

'Mostly died too, of the Bloody Flux – begging your pardon, ma'am. I use the term in the medical sense. We did have a couple of suicides, but I soon put a stop to that. These ignorant savages have strange beliefs – one being that we aimed to eat them. 'Course the crew had their fun on that score, playing them like fish, but I restrained them, seeing where it would lead.'

'Very commendable,' said Mr Loveitt acidly.

The small monkey-nut man next to him said anxiously: 'Suicides d'thee say? I don't like the sound of that. Were they shriven?' He scratched under his bag wig, knocking it askew, then straightened it in a fussy way, all the time fidgeting in his seat as if the bugs were biting there too.

'Shriven, Bob Crayshaw!' Miss Jarman brayed one of her laughs. 'You should stick to your sugar baking and not show your ignorance. Heathen savages are unlikely to belong to any church and even if they did there's no blessing for a fool who takes his own life.' She sniffed, wrinkling her nose: 'Faugh! The smell of them lies on my stomach now,' and she glared at Midnight.

The last member of the party sitting at Miss Jarman's elbow – a quietly dressed individual with the face of Punch, but with eyes like wet grapes – glanced across the table. Midnight briefly intercepted this look, then turned to the side table, exchanging a platter of carved meats for cheesecake, as if he rejected any attempt to penetrate his wall of reserve. Jess saw, but was too plagued by hunger to take much notice. She felt a sudden burst of indignation against these overstuffed bigwigs cramming themselves with food, while she sat and starved. The rouged baggage was the worst, dribbling and going on about niggers! They were all the same – never a thought for anything but their own interests. She felt a link with the blackamoor, as ignored as she was, but the feeling turned sour. She'd enough troubles of her own without shouldering his. He didn't care two straws what happened to her. She'd to look out for herself. At this moment it was her stomach that mattered. If she didn't eat and drink soon, she'd die!

The Captain beckoned to Midnight: 'More wine and ale, you black bast - ninny.' The change of term was not quick enough and he covered it with a grandiose sweep of his hand which nearly knocked over the Doctor's goblet. 'Your pardon, Doctor Plumb,' and to Midnight: 'Fill up . . . fill up . . .'

'I think we should discuss the position before drowning our sorrows,' said Mr Loveitt. 'We know some of the facts. Perhaps you can expand them and provide figures and accounts, Captain Meredith.'

'Hear, hear!' Miss Jarman hammered her knife handle on the polished oak table. 'My late respected father gave me to understand that this enterprise was full of promise. Everyone knows the Triangular Trade is guaranteed to bring home the gold. In kind if not in coin. His share was a good quarter of the capital provided for the voyage, so I expect returns.'

'No returns for any of us, ma'am,' said the Captain sadly. 'I am grieved to tell you that we have done naught but break even. No debts, mark you, but no profits neither.'

The man who looked like Punch, broke his silence: 'Proof,' he said. 'Bills of sale. Accurate accounts. Were there no slaves sold in Jamaica . . . no sugar bought? And what of your servant? Is he one of our lost profits?'

'Mr Spriggs, I am not accustomed to having my integrity questioned, or my honour smirched,' said the Captain standing up.

Jess cowered from his awful eyes, but Mr Spriggs seemed unperturbed. 'This isn't a question of integrity or honour. It's a matter of money.' He was equally cold.

'I always had me doubts; from the very first. Talked into it I was. Mind, there's Insurance, isn't there? The loss isn't total – can't be?' Bob Crayshaw said, looking up and down the table while he shifted his cutlery around as if he might find answers in the new arrangement.

'I second Joe Sprigg's request,' Miss Jarman said loudly.

'We're here for a straight account of Princess's voyage – all three sides of it; Bristol to Africa to Jamaica and back – not a social gathering, though I'm the last to turn up me nose at a good meal.' She took out an unexpected wisp of lace and linen, and dabbed at the nose.

The name 'Princess' coaxed Jess away from her preoccupation with her stomach. The Princess must be the brig, and the brig was Cap'n's kingdom. He'd said so. For a while she listened, trying to find out more about her new owner, but the conversation veered back to the voyage.

'Two hundred slaves and we made no profit?' the Doctor was saying in a jovial way that seemed out of place.

''Twas the Middle Passage at its worst, sir,' said the Captain.

Bob Crayshaw perched on the edge of his seat. 'Are you sure you didn't pack 'em too tight? Order and hygiene are most important – and boiled water. If you pack 'em like salt fish they're bound to die in shoals.'

'I know my trade, sir. If I didn't, would you have employed me to command your vessel?'

The Captain's sly answer reduced Bob Crayshaw to stuttering confusion. 'I didn't mean to . . . er . . . a sick slave is nobody's asset . . . er . . . it won't pay for an ounce of sugar . . . um . . . for the home trade . . .'

'And your servant, Captain Meredith?' asked Mr Spriggs at the end of all this.

'Bought with my own money, sir. Money from England that was nothing to do with this voyage.' Righteousness lay on the Captain's voice like castor oil on water.

'Hmm!' Mr Spriggs was not convinced. He said grudgingly: 'I'll accept that for want of proof. But surely, man, y'know there's trouble waiting for you if you try to keep any creature in bondage here? The law says all men are free in England.' He laughed sourly. 'A doubtful statement, but we have to accept it. At least you should remove his collar.'

'I don't know about removing collars,' Miss Jarman said, forestalling the Captain's outburst, 'but I'd thankee to remove the nigger. Never could abide the smell of 'em.'

'The other lad's none to savoury neither,' Bob Crayshaw complained.

The same mauve tinge that had affected the Captain's skin at the Seven Stars crept back into his pasty cheeks. He glared at Midnight and pointed at Jess.

'Take him and give him a good dowsing.'

Midnight put down the dish of cheesecake, hesitating.

'Get on with it, you black bastard. Like sparks – sparks!' said the Captain, not caring for Miss Jarman's sensitivities now.

But Midnight still waited. 'What shall he do for clothes, sir?'

'Tell the landlord to give him a shirt and breeches. I'll settle with him later. And burn those stinking rags.'

Jess pressed against the wall as if wanting to become one of the panels.

'Better to obey,' Midnight whispered as he bent over her. 'It's a wash or a flogging.' He gripped both her arms, lifting and pulling.

She went, apparently all meekness, until the door was shut behind them and they were halfway down the stairs. Then she wrenched away, meaning to run for it, but Midnight was too quick for her. He wrapped a long arm around her shoulders and neck.

'Leave go of me,' Jess said, husky and half throttled.

'Not unless you come willingly.'

'I'll not . . . I'll not . . .' She twisted and wriggled, trying to bite and when that failed, kicking back with her heels. One shoe caught his shin, but he didn't halt. Instead, he half lifted her down the rest of the stairs meaning to frogmarch her towards the door that led to the yard. 'It's you or me,' he said in her ear. 'And I don't intend taking a flogging for a white bastard.'

Jess fought more fiercely, frightened now, and the rumpus brought people out into the passage. The landlord came pushing through.

'Who's that and where are th'taking him?'

'Captain Meredith orders him to be cleansed. I take him to the yard. If you would be so good as to allow me a bucket of water, then I'll see to him. Oh, and Captain Meredith asks if you would provide shirt and breeches, to be paid for when the meeting is over.'

The landlord seemed taken aback: 'Clothes th'say?' I don't know about that.'

A small dumpy woman pushed forward. 'He can have our Bart's that he grew out of, Dan. Reckon they're of a size. I'll look un out. Have a tub of water in the kitchen. It's mortal cold for an icy drenching in the yard.' She chuckled as if the idea was highly amusing. 'The lad can scrub by the fire. He's got nothing we ain't seen afore.'

Jess hugged her arms tight across her chest. There was truth in that, but not what the silly old baggage was thinking. Oh Christmas, what was to become of her? She'd not had a bath since . . . since . . . It was too long to remember, but it wasn't the idea of being wet that mattered. She would be betrayed!

'Come along, I'll take thee.' The dumpy woman went bustling into a large stone flagged kitchen where a great fire flamed in an open fireplace and the smell of roasting meat rose from a thick flank of beef on a spit.

'Give over, lad. There's naught to fear. Th'll be cosy as a bug in a bed. Here, Dolly, give us a hand with the water tub.'

The woman called Dolly left the pastry she was rolling, wiping floury hands on a sacking apron before helping to lift the round wooden tub nearer the fire.

Jess was in a frenzy by now. Midnight's arm was like a bar of iron and all her kicking and struggling was useless. She bawled out:

'I ain't washing, not if the King himself was to beg me!'

'That ain't likely, me love,' said the dumpy woman with a shower of chuckles.

'Leave go . . . leave go . . .' squealed Jess, at last managing to swivel round to face Midnight and, burrowing her nose between his shirt buttons, reached flesh. She sunk her teeth, biting as hard as she could. His arm slackened with a painful intake of breath and she ducked back. But she wasn't free yet. There was a ripping sound as Samson's rotten shirt tore from shoulder to waist. Waistcoat and shirt rags pulled back from her shoulders along with the shift beneath, which had split like tissue paper. Then she was free. Midnight had let go. But it was too late.

The noise in the kitchen switched off as the small second she stood there half-naked seemed to lengthen into years. Captain Meredith observed her from the open door, as did Miss Jarman. They had followed the landlord into the kitchen, all three drawn by the noise.

The moment was cracked by Miss Jarman's horse laugh: 'Dammee, that's the strangest lad I ever saw!' New ship's boy did you say, Captain Meredith?'

The Captain didn't answer. His pale eyes ice-burned Jess's skin as she hastily pulled the remnants of the shirt around her. He spoke first to Jess, then to the landlord's wife.

'Lad or wench, you still stink. See that she baths, ma'am. No skimping, and I'd look kindly on it if you'd provide her with petticoats. Don't let her out of this room. She's full of sly ways and has yet to work off her debts to me.'

'Debts, Captain?' Miss Jarman came into the middle of the kitchen for a closer look at Jess, then suddenly slapping her hand down on the corner of the big floury table said: 'What d'you say to letting me pay whatever she owes? A lass of spirit. I like that . . . dammee if I don't. She can come home with me. Phoebe needs a good kitchen maid. What's her price?' She fumbled in her ample skirts, drawing out a small netted purse.

The Captain was put out. 'I've not had time to consider . . . had other plans . . . not sure . . .'

'Not sure? Never believe a man when he prevaricates about money. I insist on buying her. Half a sovereign . . . what d'you say to that?'

'I have no wish to sell,' said the Captain.

''Twas a shilling he paid for me, missus,' Jess dared to say. 'Not a penny more,' feeling the hairs stand on her arms with a fearful joy at showing him up.

'Then he's made a profit,' said Miss Jarman, winking at her. She tossed the coin at the Captain. 'Won't take no. Insist on having her.' And she marched out of the kitchen, her tall wig swaying slightly with the brisk jerky movement.

Slowly the Captain picked up the half-sovereign, and as slowly rubbed it on his sleeve. His face was terrible and Jess turned away, not able to bear such a look. Then he, too, turned and without a backward glance went out into the passage, slamming the door.

The landlord's dumpy wife began trotting about, finding a scrubbing brush and a length of rag for a towel, pausing only to say sharply: 'Get thee out then! This ain't a peep show for a nigger to watch.'

Midnight, tall and still against a background of copper

pans hanging on the wall, looked directly at Jess. She caught her breath. They were the same. Ordered about. Both of them. From morning till night. Birth till death. For always and ever.

Unwelcome tears of frustration filled her eyes. When she rubbed them clear he was no longer there.

Good riddance, she thought, scowling fiercely at the water. And devil take this lark! But there was no escape. Dolly was wedging the door handle with the back of a chair and the landlord's wife waited gleefully, scrubbing brush in hand. With slow grudging movements Jess began to remove the rest of her clothes.

Five

Miss Jarman's shabby carriage rolled up the gravelled drive between thick bushes of laurel, stopping in front of an imposing panelled door hung about with brass knockers and bell-pulls. The house was as important as the door. Looking at it, Jess thought it the grandest place she'd ever seen. It stood way up Brandon Hill in a rambling garden that in summer was full of overblown roses, but now under the dying rays of a winter sun, was a ruin of dead leaves and straggling yellow grass. She was to discover that she could see for miles from the attic windows – almost the whole of Bristol. Two rivers; spires; belching towers of the bottle factories; a web of streets scissored by the masts and sails of anchored vessels; even the distant countryside. But for the present she was lost in the wonder of her changed fortune. A little scared, very curious, ravenously hungry and ready to argue the toss with anyone after being passed from person to person like so many yards of parceled muslin.

Miss Jarman was heaving herself out of the carriage with the help of the crabbed old driver; marching up the steps and rapping on the front door shouting:

'Salt . . . SALT . . . drat the woman. PHOEBE!'

The door swung open into gloom. Miss Jarman swept in. Jess followed apprehensively.

'Where the devil were you, Salt?' Miss Jarman demanded of the tall bony female who was returning glare for glare without any sign of backing down. Her plain dress and lace cap, which seemed stuck to her iron-grey hair more by force of will than anything else, all added to her forbidding appearance. When she spoke, it was fiercely:

'Upstairs, ma'am. And stairs trouble me you may have noticed.' She closed the front door, and from her rocking walk Jess realised that one of her legs must be a good deal shorter than the other.

'Hmm!' said Miss Jarman, crossing the gloomy hall and opening another door.

Jess wasn't going to be left with the eyes of all the dead Jarmans (if that's who they were) looking down on her from their elaborate gold-framed portraits. She scuttled through the door and found herself in a long drawing-room choked with old-fashioned furniture.

Salt came swaying after, shouting in her strident voice: 'Not there! Servants this way . . .'

But Miss Jarman dismissed her with: 'In a minute, Salt. I'll send the purchase to the kitchen when Miss Phoebe and I have examined it.'

Salt withdrew mumbling, and Jess fumed. 'Purchase' was she? She'd give 'em their money's worth!

'Phoebe!' Miss Jarman went to a wing chair by the black marble fireplace and shook the middle-aged woman sleeping there.

She sat up, flustered, curls and cap slipping; her round blue eyes misty with sleep. 'What's to do? Who . . . oh Harriet, you startled me. And who's that?' As she talked, she tried smoothing her crumpled lilac gown, then retying the fichu round her shoulders, succeeding in neither.

'Who indeed! You know as much as me – or nearly. It's something I picked up in the Trow.' Miss Jarman sat down with a thump in the matching wing chair on the other side of the fireplace.

'*What?*'

'In the Llandogger Trow,' snapped Miss Jarman. 'And I've asked it nary a word till we got here, so as you could hear the story as well. Can't stand repetition.'

She eased off her shoes and held her white stockinged feet to the blaze, spreading her toes and raising a smell of toasting cheese. 'Ah . . . that's better. Been wanting to get them off for hours. Pinch me something shocking.'

Phoebe Jarman stared at Jess with almost as much caution as Jess eyed her. She smiled slightly, a nervous smile that held kindliness. Jess didn't respond. She wasn't going to give her smiles away – not till she'd fixed her position, and certainly not to an ugly pock-marked thing like Miss Phoebe with her beaky nose and whiskery chin . . . though she did have nice eyes.

Harriet Jarman pointed at Jess. 'Right. Fire away. Name!'

'Jess,' Jess said reluctantly.

'Jess what?'

'No name.'

'Jess no-name! That's a nice bit of double-barrelled lying. Quick. Out with it or I'll have your skin for a cigar case.'

'I ain't lying!' Jess said, stung. 'Peters is what they give me 'cause I was born in St Peter's Hospital . . . the Old Mint . . . the Poorhouse.' She took particular trouble over this list of names, spitting out each one like unwanted orange pips. 'Me ma went and dropped me there and died without so much as a word. So there I were – a Christmas present for the parish. The old bleed – overseer called me Jess after his dog as died that day. I'll have Jess, but I ain't having Peters.' She stuck her chin in the air and glared – underneath shaking as if she had an ague.

Miss Jarman glared back. 'We'll pass over your doubtful history and come to the interesting part. What were you doing dressed as a lad and in Captain Meredith's company?' She screwed up her face at the name as if it left a nasty taste in her mouth, adding: 'Can't abide that man. Fishy ... devious. Father must have been out of his mind to employ him.'

'Harriet, how can you say such a thing! You wouldn't have spoken so if he'd been alive,' Miss Phoebe protested.

'Well he isn't. Our affairs are in my hands now and I'll speak as I see things. And what I see clearly is that those things aren't right. Capital squandered. Prospects drowned. We can't afford such a loss. I tell you I'm not satisfied with that pesky voyage.'

'Nothing but bad comes out of such trade. No one should buy and sell human souls.' Miss Phoebe's voice wavered, but whether with indignation or fear of her sister, Jess couldn't be sure. Certainly she jumped when Harriet barked:

'Rubbish! Sentimental wish-wash! Everyone knows it's an act of kindness rescuing those niggers from the heathen savagery of their native land. I'd like to know where you'd be now if it wasn't for Father's African interests. Not in this house. And not fed and clothed in the style to which you're accustomed.'

'There are many of the Friends who live comfortably without ...'

'Friends! Whose friends? Not mine. Quakers!' Harriet's scorn was searing. 'I'm not going through all that again. We've had it out and I've said what I've said and that's the finish.'

Whatever the old baggage had said, it must have been thorny, Jess thought. Both of them looked roused. Miss Phoebe's pitted cheeks were quite pink and there were tears in her eyes. Still, it had made them forget her. Perhaps she'd not be required to answer.

She was wrong. Miss Jarman never forgot anything. A lesson Jess was to learn time and again in the coming weeks.

'Get on with it, Jess Peters. And look sharp. I've work to do.'

Jess's cheeks flamed. 'Jess Peters'! 'A purchase'! Painted old crow! She looked no better than the whores haunting Christmas Steps and Marsh Street. Worse in fact. No man 'ud want a lay like that!

But she couldn't escape the watchful waiting eyes and muttered sullenly: ''Tis easier working in a tavern dressed as a boy. The men don't tamper with thee. Landlord give me breeches an' that. She glanced quickly, then away, to see if her lies had been accepted. They had, but the grilling wasn't over.

'Well – and how did you come by the Captain?' Miss Jarman tapped impatiently on the arm of her chair with yellow stained fingers.

Jess hung her head, mumbling: 'Climbed on the brig.'

'What's that? Speak up. Raise your head. Climbed up what if you please?'

'The mooring rope.'

Miss Jarman's sharp eyes bored like drills. 'Because?'

Jess looked up then, defiantly. Hating these overstuffed upper-class bitches. 'Took a loaf, that's what. I were that hungry. If th'guts'd been griping and grinding like as if a corkscrew were twisting there, thee'ud have done the same. I ain't a thief by nature. Some folk just don't get a choice. I had to hide. They 'ud've strung me up if they'd taken me.'

The room suddenly wavered, melting and reforming only to melt again. From a long way off she heard a voice say: 'Green as a bit of ripe Stilton . . .' and then the room disappeared.

When she came to, the acrid tingling of sal volatile was in her nostrils. Salt was peering at her and Miss Phoebe was chafing her hand.

'She's round, ma'm,' Salt said in her angry voice, and under her breath; 'Blessed if I know what the world's coming to . . . serving wenches falling about and being propped in chairs as if they were gentry.'

Jess looked round. She was in a chair. A wing chair. Miss Phoebe's!

'Feeling a little better, my dear?' Miss Phoebe asked.

She'd never been anybody's dear before. The face was ugly but the inquiring smile kind. A very tiny crack appeared in Jess's armour. Not such an old cow after all. She smiled wistfully; all the longing coming with such a rush that tears squeezed on to her cheeks. She rubbed them away with an angry fist. She was a fool to let anyone get round her. How long before she learned that folk'll always take advantage of weakness?

'My dear child,' said Miss Phoebe, unwittingly driving in another wedge.

'Oh don't fuss so, Phoebe!' Harriet, equally unwittingly, saved Jess from bursting into tears. 'Take her in the kitchen, Salt, and fill her up with gruel or some such thing.'

'Not gruel!' Jess said, goaded unendurably by the memory of her last meal.

'Th'can eat what th'bist given and be thankful,' Salt said grimly, helping her to her feet.

In the end she ate the remains of yesterday's mutton pie with small beer to swill it down and an orange to follow that was so juicy rivulets ran down her chin into the worn neck frill of the landlord's wife's cast-off blouse.

'Here!' Salt handed her a cloth from the rail over the wide kitchen fireplace. 'Th'manners need a polish.'

'Never got no teaching,' Jess said, feeling bolder with food inside.

'Well, th'can start now. Miss Jarman's a stickler for neat ways.'

Remembering the dropped meat lumps and dribbling sauce, Jess raised her eyebrows. Salt scowled.

'Whatever th'thinks, th'd better mind th'self. Miss Jarman's gaffer now old Mister's dead.'

'She's a rum 'un,' Jess said.

'Saucy baggage! Don't know what got into her to bring home such a guttersnipe.' Salt went to take a huge apple pie from the oven set in the chimney place, releasing cinnamon sweetness.

Jess stuck out her tongue at the broad back and said in demure tones: 'No, but her is . . . no offense meant.' (Oh but that pie smelt good!)

Salt's great shoulders twitched as she turned the pie and put it back, but she didn't deny it. When she straightened up, her face was red, perhaps from the fire. 'Ain't no flies on her though,' she said. 'Th'mind what I say and th'll doubtless find there's no better place than Jarman House.'

A place? Jess looked round the big kitchen; at the dresser full of blue and white china; the copper kettle hanging steaming over the fire; the tubs and jugs and iron pans; the rough whitewashed walls and the big sash window looking out on to a rising kitchen garden. She'd never dreamed of getting work in a place like this. A small flame of hope lit. She snuffed it out. But it was to burn again in the candlelit drawing-room where the two sisters sat opposite each other after supper in a warm red glow of port, firelight and reflections from the red velvet curtains drawn against night air.

'Nothing but bare boards, you say?' Miss Jarman asked, taking up an ivory hand on a long stick and scratching under her wig, starting a snowstorm of powder.

Jess nodded. 'And an empty keg or two.'

'You're sure?'

'Said so, didn't I?'

'No need to be pert, miss. Just for that you can start again, from the moment you climbed up the mooring rope.'

Jess sighed and blew out her cheeks. The day had been very long and packed to bursting. Now with her belly tight as a balloon, all she wanted to do was sleep and sleep and sleep. But this old crow had that get-on-with-it look, and if she wanted this place, which she did . . . Lordy how she did! . . . she'd have to knuckle under. No more cheek. Be bright. Be careful. Suppressing a huge yawn, she went over her morning's adventures on the Princess for the fourth time.

'Handbolted to a nigger!' Miss Jarman said when she'd finished. 'Not to be countenanced.'

'Harriet, you're too narrow. These Africans are human – equal with us in the eyes of the Lord,' said Phoebe.

'Then the Lord need spectacles.'

'Harri . . .ET! I won't listen to such blasphemy.' Miss Phoebe got up. It was the first time Jess had been aware of seeing her standing. Small and birdlike with papery skin on her bird's claws, her scarred anxious face, pink-rimmed eyes blinking rapidly with emotion, she was unimpressive. There was something almost pathetic about the way she was striving for authority which she hadn't got and never would have.

Pheobe went on: 'You mustn't talk like that about people. They *are* people after all. Just because they're black . . . I mean . . . making them slaves is like condemning them . . . to . . .' Words deserted her, leaving her hands flapping as a substitute. As a last gesture of independence she moved towards the door.

'Oh sit down, Phoebe! You take everything so black and white,' Harriet said.

But Phoebe wasn't ready to give in yet. She made an inadequate attempt to neaten her cap, then fidgeted with her cuffs, keeping her back to her sister. 'Not right,' she managed. 'Can't stay and listen to another attack . . . on my . . . my . . .'

Miss Jarman sniffed heavily, took another mouthful of port and when it had gone down said testily: 'We've much to talk over y'know that. Decisions to take.'

Phoebe didn't move.

'Dammee woman, how can I set my mind to anything with you in a tiz? Y'know how it vexes me.'

'What part do I ever play in any of your decisions?' Phoebe asked.

If there was an answer, none was given. Jess wondered uncomfortably whether she was expected to move out of the way and let the old ditherer through, or side with the Law and her own interests. She didn't budge, but was slightly shaken by the trace of tears on Phoebe's sparse lashes. It wasn't a battle for top dog after all. Faint and incredible, the thought flitted in to her mind – P'raps the old crow cares what happens to folk like the Cap'n's nigger? Might even care about me!

'Are y'going to stand there like Lot's wife, Phoebe? Come now . . . y'know I need a good listener, and you are a good listener.' The last words came grudgingly.

There was a hint of a smile on Miss Phoebe's face as she went quietly back to her seat. Jess waited for her to make something out of her small success, but she didn't and sat with folded hands looking into the ever-changing flames licking around the coal.

Miss Jarman, apparently recovered, opened a carved box on the table beside her chair, took out a small cigar, bit off the end and spat it into the fire.

Jess was rivetted, the last of her fatigue fled.

'Don't gawp, miss! Light a spill for me. There . . . in the hearth. If you're to work here there are certain things you must know.' She puffed while Jess held the lighted spill steady. 'My habits, my opinions and Miss Phoebe's housekeeping system. Learn 'em, fit yourself round 'em and no one'll turn you away.'

Jess blew out the spill. Her heart was bumping and hope had come back, though this new gaffer was tricky as a fox and probably just as sly.

Miss Jarman went on: 'What I won't stomach is thieving, hypocrisy, canting men, niggers, or my servants getting into the family way. Understand?'

Jess glanced at Miss Phoebe to see how she was reacting to the bit about niggers. No visible sign, except a slight frown. There was much to learn about her an'all. Folk weren't always like their words.

The fire suddenly crackled and spat sparks. Harriet Jarman sat erect as if the noise had helped her solve whatever had been troubling her. 'A Frolic! What better for our purpose.' She looked at her sister who seemed as mystified as Jess. 'A few tables of cards – quadrille, limited loo . . . yes, and a good supper. Plenty of liquor. There's the two kegs from Moonshine Jake – gin and rum – and there's a fresh pipe of port. We'll get more sherry . . . ease their tongues. Meredith, Loveitt, Plumb . . . all the syndicate. Now then . . .' She began some complicated reckoning on her fingers while Phoebe and Jess watched in mutual astonishment. 'Wednesday today. Thursday . . . Friday . . . and Mr Goschalk from the Insurance won't call till next Tuesday – so Saturday week it is!'

'Never enough time, Harriet. All the preparations. You can't mean . . .' Phoebe relapsed into little disturbed 'ohs' rubbing her thin fingers and slithering to the edge of her chair, while Jess wondered what in the name of the Devil a syndicate was, and if a Frolic would be as jolly as it sounded. Probably not, remembering the pot-bellied crab-faced lot at the Trow.

The days flew by; a confusion of rain, new faces, gossip, enormous meals and endless tasks – some new, some well-known. Jess was given all the floor scrubbing and lugging of coals, sharing with fat giggly Sally Dade, the housemaid, dusting, washing up, bedmaking and carrying hot-water jugs to the bedrooms. There were other more unusual tasks – warming the Bible in front of the fire ready for Miss Phoebe's daily reading, and putting a bowl of mustard and water under the table so that Miss Jarman could soak her feet during breakfast.

All these things filled her attention. Samson, Will Peg, Garty Jenks grew smaller in her mind. It was another world she was in, a world of promise that was even better when the grey weather lifted on the following Wednesday. Jess's spirits rose with the sun. She whistled, hitching up her skirt and petticoats so she could run more easily down the tradesman's path to the gate. She was not hurrying to fetch the ribbons for Miss Phoebe's new cap which was being made especially for the Frolic. She ran because it was being made especially for the Frolic. She ran because it was impossible to walk. Already she was slotting into her new existence. Hard work, ample food and a neat change of clothes into the bargain. Life was good. It went on being good to the bottom of the path and all the way into the road. Then everything changed.

'Will Pegg!' she breathed.

'Alive and kicking – same as th'self.'

'What are th'doing here?' She could hardly get out the question.

'On an errand. Returning some hinges to the big house yonder. Samson mended 'em.'

Weasel eyes looking at her. Rat face. Spindle shanks and thick red hands. One on her shoulder now. She went to shrug it off.

'Now ain't that friendly,' Will said and slid an arm round her waist, pulling her to him. 'Samson wouldn't like to know as th'd got all high and mighty working in such a grand place.'

'Don't work there,' Jess said.

'Liar! I've seen thee.'

'Th'been prying like always!'

'Ah come on, Jess! Thee ain't in no place to talk about prying.' She went very red, and seeing he'd scored, Will added slyly: 'I ain't going to make trouble, leastways not if th'bist sensible. After all we've been mates, working alongside at the smithy. No need to put on airs.'

'Leave go of me!' She couldn't cloak her antagonism which was all the worse for the element of truth in what he said.

'Listen, Lady Muck. Th'can do summat for me and if th'doesn't Samson shall know where th'lives. He don't love thee since Garty moaned so he had to pay back the two shilling given for thee. Not that he can't afford it, but the shame riled un. He'd be glad to thrash thee senseless.'

Jess knew that to be true. 'What do th'want?' she asked hopelessly.

'That's better.' Will smiled, giving her a squeeze. 'Th'bist a right tarty bit of stuff. Never fancied thee afore, but now . . .'

'Get on with it,' Jess said icily.

'A shilling . . . no, two shilling for a wager I've in mind.' He laughed. 'Two for old time's sake. There's to be a cock-main at the Galleon pit tonight and I reckon to go, but I ain't going skint.'

'I ain't got two shilling,' Jess said. She felt sick and cold. The new life that seemed so full of promise lay dying at her feet. She tried attack. 'And who are thee to threaten? There's still them nails th'took.'

'No trade,' Will said. Th'bist a better bargain than year-old nails. Who's going to believe thee anyway?'

'I ain't got money,' Jess repeated desperately.'

'Get it then and I'll see thee tonight. Half after eight at the Galleon,' Will said heartlessly.

'I tell you I ain't got a bleedin' farthing and even if I had I'm expected to be working. There's the fires to care for and pots to be washed.' She was almost choking with despair, seeing that none of this was making a whisker of difference.

'A clever wench like thee'll think of summat,' Will said with a grin. 'Tell th'what – if I wins I'll treat thee. Can't say fairer than that, except if th'bist good to me as well I might even give thee back the two shilling.' And he walked away down the hill.

Raging, she watched until he was out of sight. The ribbon money burned in her hand. No. No. NO! And yet he'd talked about giving it back if he won and if she was good to him. She shuddered, knowing what he suggested. Knowing also his hinted promise was likely to be so much dust.

She opened her hand and looked at the two silver coins. Sixpence short. But still he might accept it. No. No. NO! With panic inside her she set off in Will's footsteps towards the town, sobbing.

She was back within the hour, her face shiny with dried tears, her eyes red-rimmed. She'd worked on that, rubbing them hard.

'Lordy, what's amiss?' Salt said as Jess came running into the kitchen.

There was no difficulty in bursting into tears again. She was really upset. 'Money . . . lost . . .' she hiccupped.

'Here now, give it over. Lost th'say? Th'half-witted drab! How did it happen?'

But Jess hid her face, moaning into her hands with all the artistry she could summon. Salt shook her shoulder and when that made no difference, dragged her to her feet and propelled her to the small book-lined room known as the study. The sisters were both there, Harriet behind a stout oak desk; Phoebe beside her. They were doing their accounts.

'Now then,' Salt said, giving Jess a little push: 'Tell what th'told me!'

Jess began to shake and the sobs she'd encouraged broke out with fresh vigour and real conviction.

'Mercy on us, child. Whatever's the matter?' Miss Phoebe asked, full of concern.

Jess made a vague gesture with her hands: 'I dropped th'money, miss, and it rolled . . . oh . . . it went bouncing along . . . like little silver wheels straight down the crack between them flaps as covers cellars. In Wine Street, it were, near the Corn Market.' She couldn't resist embroidering the description, seeing all in her mind as if it had really happened. She looked up at Phoebe with an anguished expression that was nearly honest repentance. 'Oh miss, what must th'think of me. It was that careless . . . oh . . .' She managed another sob, face again in her hands.

'How did you come to drop the money?' Harriet asked

brusquely.

'Someone bumped me, ma'am. Caught me foot I did and nearly fell,' Jess said, muffled by her hands. 'Oh . . .'

'That's quite enough dramatics.'

'Harriet, she's upset.' Phoebe said.

'I'm not surprised, trying it on like that. She's right to be upset. She knows what's coming.'

'Oh ma'm, don't be hard on me. I know what th'must be thinking, but cut me heart out I never stole nothing. Don't turn me off. Take it out of me wages.' She knew she was taking a risk. Nobody had so much as breathed the word 'Wages'. Oh Christmas, let the old baggage be convinced! It was true. It was. It would be, if her suggestion was accepted. In her frantic anxiety she began rubbing her eyes and then her dripping nose as if trying to flatten both into her skull.

'Should send you packing,' Harriet said.

'Harriet, it's my money she lost. I believe her. Give her another chance, do.'

Harriet made a grunting sound that meant she'd given in under protest and Jess didn't wait for any other sign.

'Thankee, miss . . . thankee both. I'll not forget th'goodness. Th'won't be sorry. I'll see to that,' she said, this time meaning every word.

Six

'I'll wager ten shillings on the Brasseywing. It's got as bright and fierce an eye as I've seen this side the Avon.'

'Make it a guinea, Mr Lambert sir. 'Tain't like thee to make such small stakes.'

'Needs must, Harry. I'm short of the ready, but when I win I'll lay a bigger stake. I intend doing great things tonight . . . great things. Right, Randall?' James Lambert removed his tricorn hat and ran fingers through his unruly hair. His face was flushed and there was a slight unsteadiness about him.

The man called Randall smiled coolly and picked imaginary foreign bodies off the galloon braiding of his immaculate dark green coat. 'By the Lord, Jimmie, you always did have rose-edged ambitions, but like sunsets they fade.' He took a linen kerchief from an inner pocket, held it to his think hooked nose and addressed the bet collector: 'What's the name of the fine Black-Red?'

'Damocles, sir. Give 'em high-flown names these days. There were a cock I saw out at Kingswood – naught but a shake-bag it were. Lucifer Angelwing, the owner called it, if th'pleases! I said to him, "Tom", I said . . . Tom was the owner, sir . . .'

'Ten guineas on Damocles.' Randall cut across the story. 'I advise you to back him as well, Jimmie.'

'The Brasseywing's the better fighter, I'll wager. Look at his stance. Beak's been filed to needle sharpness. Good spurs too. Finest steel.'

'James . . . James, you always were gullible.' Randall shook his head sadly.

'I'm right I tell you!'

'Like you were at the tables last night and the night before that?'

James Lambert began to bluster. 'A run of bad luck, no more. Could happen to anyone. Temporary bad luck. I'll swear to it.'

'To the tune of two hundred guineas? I tell you, back Damocles!'

James puffed out a great breath, digging his hands deep into the empty pockets of his coat. 'Very well, if you're so sure, advance me five and I'll take your advice.'

'Done!' Randall smiled again with the hint of mockery, settled the bet and turning away with his kerchief pressed even more firmly to his nose, moved into the cockpit where the cock-masters were preparing their birds for the fight.

James Lambert turned too, but towards the doors opening on to the yard and air. The heat and stench of the converted barn was suddenly unbearable. He felt faint and nauseous. He had to get out before he spewed, and pushed through the crowd, jostling Jess who was on her way in.

She recognised him immediately, but though his gaze passed over her there was no recognition. Not that she expected there would be. A tidy wench was unlikely to revive memories of a ragged boy aboard the *Princess*. Another time she would have followed him out of curiosity, but now she had only one thing in mind. Having risked everything coming here, she wasn't going to leave without finding Will Pegg. She scanned the barn, but was too short to see much, especially in the uncertain light.

People were squeezing towards the raised pit to get a better look at the fighting cocks. Two were already straining from the hands of their masters, neck ruffs erect as they waited for the moment of release on to the sawdust-strewn floor. Others were in lidded baskets until it was their turn; more tied in sacks; a few buttoned into deep pockets. All round was a babble of talk about odds and form. All round, the rich stink of sweat, urine, spilled ale, even a trace of potpourri. But no Will.

Jess elbowed through the crowd, aiming for the opposite side of the barn where a ladder led to a hayloft. Reaching it she climbed a few rungs and looked over the heads of the people and the cockpit where a double ring of candles hung low on iron chains from the rafters, spreading a brilliant pool of light. Beyond – the shadowy barn doors, closed. The place was thronging with all sorts – rough working men, sailors, neatly dressed tradespeople, a few dandies. One in front caught her eye. A regular blood, with his fine clothes, holding his nose as he leaned towards the cocks. She sniggered. He'd do better watching his pockets!

Then she forgot him because Will had come in. She knew his shape though his face was in shadow. He was looking round. Looking for her. Jess slid from the ladder. It was important to position himself within easy reach of the doors before letting him see her, in case she had to bolt. She knew him too well to imagine he'd let her get away easily, even when he learned there was money. No point in pleading either, though that was what she had in mind. But she must ask; beg even, or he'd be knocking on the kitchen door at Jarman House, asking the Lord knew what favours.

The crowd was more impenetrable than ever. Even at the edges it was difficult pushing through.

'Mind thy elbows, th'scratty little varmint!'

Jess ignored the protest and pushed on, managing to keep close to the wall and surfacing not two feet from the doors.

'Will!'

A smile of real pleasure spread over his mean face as he caught sight of her. Admiration too. The way he was looking her over made her want to run.

'Th'came after all. Sensible. I always thought thee a fly un.' He came towards her quickly. 'Where's the money? I needs it for a wager on the Brasseywing.'

'Well hid,' Jess said. 'It'll take a minute to get at it.'

'What do th'mean?'

'In me garter at the top of me stocking,' Jess said. 'I'll have it ready for the next bout. This un's just starting. Look!'

There was a raucous shout and a flurry of wings as the cockmasters threw their birds at one another. They met breasts and heads together, and tumbled to the floor, pecking and clawing viciously, the Brasseywing on top, but only for a moment. There were shouts and bellows of encouragement for one and the other. Jess couldn't see except when the birds rose up an instant only to fall back, this time with Damocles mounted and digging in his spurs. There was a bird-screech and a swell of shouting. Jess was glad she couldn't see. She hadn't much stomach for torn flesh or pecked eyes streaming blood. But Will pushed into the crowd for a better view, pulling her with him.

'Go on . . . go on . . . kill un . . .' He was pinching her arm in his excitement, turning for a moment when she complained. 'What's th'fancy, Jess? Brasseywing's a fine un ain't he? Come on feller . . . that's it . . .'

Jess tried to pull away, but it was no good. She'd known all along she'd be made to stay and watch. Lord above, what was she going to say to Salt when she got back – and to the old baggages?

'Leave go, Will – if th'want th'money.' She tried lifting her skirt to fish under it for the pocket hangin over her petticoat. The lie to Will had been second nature. She didn't want him to know all her secrets.

'That's it . . . kick un . . . NO!' bawled Will, glued to the fight and relaxing his grip.

Jess found the money, pressed it into his hand and took a backward look to see if there was the chance of a run for the doors. Will, roused by the feel of money followed her glance. They both saw Garty Jenks at the same time. More than that – Jess saw the nod and wink exchanged. For a moment she was speechless, then she fairly spat out:

'Bugger! Th'two-faced, wall-eyed, shifty bugger! For a paper of pins I'd scratch thy eyes out! How much has he paid thee? Don't stand there grinning like a stuck pig . . . tell us. How much?'

'Two shilling, same as afore. Only now there's a profit.' He held up his clenched fist, apparently unaware of the missing sixpence.

Jess felt like ramming it down his throat. And to think she'd pulled the wool over Miss Phoebe's eyes! Jesus . . . it was enough to make anyone spit blood! Phoebe was a doddering fool, but trusting – the only one in years to offer a kind word. 'Ooooh!' and Jess released a hissing breath of fury.

The crowd was getting to a fever pitch of excitement, Will among them. The cockpit was littered with feathers and spattered with blood. One bird was down. The other clawed into it, mercilessly pecking while its prey squawked with weakening jabs of its beak. There was a trickle of scarlet, a roar from the crowd and the Brasseywing lay dead. Still Damocles worried and pecked, coated with blood and frantic with an apparently unquenchable desire to kill and kill again. Through a sudden gap between heads Jess saw and felt sick. She pulled away from Will who'd slipped an arm round her waist. She reached the door, but got no further because Garty was leaning against it.

'Let me out!' she said, too hot with anger to feel fear.

He grinned in a casual way, but didn't move. 'Why?'

''Cause I asked, that's why.' She tried hooking her fingers round the door and pulling, but he only laughed and grabbing her, dragged her to him, kissing the part nearest his face, which happened to be the base of her neck. 'Now th'can go out,' he said and went with her into the shadow-filled yard; one long arm guiding her with relentless force past the lighted windows of the inn, past the well and a small cart, past James Lambert walking shakily towards the back door of the inn, to a dark corner behind a group of empty ale kegs. Will followed not two paces behind.

*

In the kitchen of the Galleon, Midnight crouched over the blazing heat of the fire. His front was toasting, but icicles seemed to be lying along his back. If he lived to be a hundred, he'd never get used to this evil oozing cold. A memory of hot suns, with grass burned brown and ripe plantains yellowing the trees of home, touched him. Passionate homesickness rose and buffeted him harder than it had done for months. How long since he left? Fifty moons? Sixty? He couldn't recall and somehow this was worse than anything. Certainly before he was made a man. Now he never would be. He'd never see his homeland again; never see parent, sister . . .

'Get out of the road th'dozy black lump . . . cooking

th'self like any cannibal!' The fat cook pushed him out of the way, coming to turn a pan of potatoes roasting under spitted beef.

Midnight wandered to the open door, wondering how long Captain Meredith would stay in this place. Across the courtyard the barn door pulled back, letting out light and people, but he noticed them only vaguely, his mind absorbed with a vivid picture of the fog-bound deck. He saw the moving mouth of the man so nearly dead; the stain on the waistcoat, and felt a strengthening of the foreboding that had never left him. Had anyone else been witness? His friend Mr Lambert perhaps?

The thought was scarcely born before James Lambert himself appeared, hardly more than a shadow in the dusk, but unmistakable as he walked past the pile of kegs. Imagination and reality fused and for a second the sense of foreboding intensified. James Lambert hesitated, turning towards the kegs, from behind which came the sounds of a scuffle. There was a scream that brought echoes from the past, but it was a woman's scream, followed by shouts and curses. The kegs shifted, teetered, fell! Behind, three figures were struggling. Midnight tensed, seeing James Lambert try to push between; seeing two of them turn on him.

'Always the same when there's a cock-main,' grumbled the cook as he prodded the potatoes. 'Always some bastard ready for a scrap.' But his only audience was the stone-deaf woman washing up. Midnight had left the doorway and was already running across the yard. He launched himself at the taller of the two men, dragging him back. Deflecting the blow aimed at James Lambert's head with his left arm, he drove his right fist short but hard into the man's mouth, loosening teeth and skinning his knuckles.

The man grunted and staggered back. Midnight spun

round to see the other – broad and stunted – lower his massive head and ram it into James Lambert's stomach. They collapsed together on the ground. James winded; his attacker sprawling over him punching, and thrusting with his thick trunk in a way that prevented any return blow.

Behind him Will Pegg shouted through bloody lips: 'Look out for th'self, Garty . . . take the black bugger. I'll settle the other.'

Garty saw Midnight and got up. He blundered forward, punching wildly. Midnight swung his left arm with all the force and weight of his body – a hammer-blow on the man's right cheekbone. Garty's head jerked violently sideways; he lurched, stumbled, almost fell, then seemed to find his balance again. Panting and cursing with pain and rage he came back, head lowered. This time Midnight moved aside and grasping him round the back of the neck as he passed, flung him headlong into the gathering crowd.

Uproar then, and shouts of: 'The nigger's got th'measure, short-arse . . . fist like a cannon ball . . . who'll have twopence on him to win . . .' as the crowd heaved Garty to his feet, helped him round and sent him flying back towards Midnight.

In the corner where she had fallen when Garty hit her, Jess crooked her knees then slowly pulled herself up. Fingermarks stood in raised weals across one cheek and her left eye was half closed. Her head throbbed and burned. She peered at the men fighting, for the life of her not able to think why anyone would come to her rescue.

Randall's thoughts were different. Aloof from the sweating mob, he watched with keen interest, seeing Midnight's poise, his speed, his economy of movement.

Will Pegg yelled again: 'Look out for th'self, Garty . . . kill un!' but it was too late.

Midnight turned gently from a blow that grazed his ribs

and brought his right fist down, short and deadly, on to the side of his stubbled jaw. Garty's legs collapsed and he fell to the ground, a twitching moaning heap. There was a purple swelling rising on his broken cheekbone.

A cheer went up with only a single shout of 'Shame!' – and recognising his defeat, Will turned and fled without carrying out his threat.

Slipping his arm under James Lambert's shoulders, Midnight asked: 'Are you much hurt, sir?'

James sat up painfully. 'I'll live. It was foolish to take on two, but I couldn't stomach what they were at.'

'You always did have a gallant streak, Jimmie,' Randall said, skirting the crowd. 'Luck was on your side for once in the form of this remarkable pugilist, this amazing pair of fists!' He touched Midnight's arm lightly.

'Midnight . . .' James said, getting up but still hunched over, 'a friend indeed!' then noticing blood staining the white shirt cuff: 'Your knuckles, man . . .'

'It's nothing.' Midnight put his hand behind his back.

'That is ill-considered nonsense,' Randall said, taking Midnight's arm and examining the cut and the swelling. 'Any man with such a punch should guard against infection. See that you bathe the injury and apply witch-hazel. You can flex your fingers I hope?'

Midnight spread and clenched his hand.

'No bones broken. Good . . . good.'

James said with sick irritation: 'Leave the man alone, Randall, he's not made of eggshell.'

Randall looked at him impatiently. 'He saves you from a beating with remarkable ease and skill, yet you remain as blind and dull-witted as an earthworm. No wonder you always lose.'

James closed his eyes wearily. 'What are you talking about?'

'The gift of a prizefighter. He's dropped like a ripe plum into your hand and you fail to recognise the possibilities. Stake him and you'll make your fortune.'

James opened his eyes, looking at Randall uncertainly. 'Stake him? You know I'm cleaned out.'

'You've a neat hundred now Damocles has won,' Randall said with a short laugh. 'That should prove I've an eye for a winner.'

'But he's Captain Meredith's slave.'

'There's no such thing as a slave in England. He's a servant and servants can hire themselves to whom they please. Give him board and lodging, proper training, the right food . . . why, you've pure gold tipped into your lap! Take hold, man. Take him down to the Hatchett. Matt will provide everything for half your hundred.'

It was James's turn to laugh. A hollow sick sound. 'You haven't met Captain Meredith, Randall. A pleasure yet to come.'

Ignored and forgotten, Jess moved closer, fascinated by the way things were turning out. Listening to the conversation in which Midnight had no part, she felt a sudden pity for him which increased the sense of gratitude already there, and was slightly surprised when the foppish Randall asked him a direct question:

'Who taught you to punch like that?'

'No one.'

'But that power, your cool head, the artful way you played him?'

Midnight shrugged, looking over the faultless green shoulder at Jess. 'Where survival is all, you learn or die.'

Jess heard and knew in an absent way that he was speaking to her, but all attention was on Captain Meredith, framed in the doorway of the inn. Midnight turned as the Captain moved through light beams spreading from the windows across the yard. To both his presence was chilling. The word of thanks that Jess had ready remained unspoken.

Unaware, Randall was saying urgently: 'What would you say if I was to arrange myself? No backyard brawls, I assure you . . . well-matched, well-controlled prizefights. The sport is in need of a worthy champion.'

Still watching the Captain, Midnight said: 'I am allowed no right to choose. A slave must do as his master bids.'

Very close to him now, Jess reached out impulsively and touched his sleeve. She had a need to thank him. There was a gleam of white teeth and the white rim of his eyes. She smiled back, painfully. And ran.

Seven

Jarman House was humming with preparations for the Frolic. Jess felt it was like watching an upturned ants' nest. Everyone scurrying around in a kind of frantic muddled order. Sally Dade trundled backwards and forwards in and out of the kitchen carrying table linen, candlesticks, silver and cut-glassware in a bath of sweat and giggles, while Mrs Stocks, who usually only came once in five weeks for an orgy of washing, wept silently into the pan of onions she was skinning. Between roaring fire and loaded table Salt moved grimly and with great determination, roasting, baking, conjuring such delectable smells that Jess kept having to swallow the saliva that filled her mouth.

'That's the tables done,' Sally said, coming in with a great draught that stirred the fire and puffed curls of smoke from under the mantel-shelf.

'Th'd best see to the port then, instead of blowing about under my feet,' Salt snapped. 'Get Hawkins to go down in the cellar and help thee, and mind th'don't get up to any pranks.'

'With Mr Hawkins!' Sally burst into a such a fit of giggling, Jess thought she'd explode from the tight lacings of her bodice. 'He's past it, Mrs Salt!'

'Saucy trollop!' was the only retort, accompanied by the hollow slap of gravy being beaten with a wooden spoon.

Sally went out, still chuckling, leaving Jess planted in front of a steaming tub, sleeves rolled up, arms red to the elbow, washing pots, pans, cutlery – more pots, more pans (burnt this time), more cutlery, until she felt like tipping the whole lot on to the floor. She didn't of course. Her place held on a thread. Only the nearness of the Frolic had saved her from being turned out that disastrous night. The memory of the terrible moment she had come face to face with Salt rolled over her. Creeping up the backstairs on her return from the Galleon, she'd foolishly thought she was safe. She could hear Salt's acid voice now; sniff her scent of vanilla. And after . . . those two harpies poking and prying and issuing threats as if they were God . . . oh . . .

'Jess Peters, stop th'daydreaming. There's work in plenty if we're to be finished on time. Th'bist in enough trouble without lazing.

The harsh reminder was enough to set Jess resentfully scouring again. She knew that she was safe until the Frolic was over. There hadn't been any time to find a new skivvy, and a skivvy was vital if the evening was to be a success. Someone had to go round with the coals, wash up, sweep, scrub, polish, fetch and carry.

The longcase clock in the hall began its silver chiming and Sally with Hawkins came back with several dusty port bottles.

'Lord-a-mercy it's six already!' Salt said, attacking a saddle of mutton with a terrible knife and sculpturing the meat with precision. 'We'll be needing more brandy from the cellar but it can wait awhile. Baste them pheasants, Sally, and Mr Hawkins can tap the keg of porter.'

Jess had noticed that she never spoke directly to the old man. He was here on sufferance as coach driver and odd jobber. Men, it seemed, were scarcely tolerated in the Jarman household and Mr Hawkins was nothing but a leftover from the days when old Mr Jarman was alive. As she slopped about in the cooling water, Jess pondered over this peculiarity. P'raps the old baggages had been crossed in love. A lover dying of smallpox – Miss Phoebe was scarred from it. A kiss between them and death to follow. She slapped a shining pan on top of a precarious tower in the draining tub. More like nobody had ever asked to marry either of 'em! Soured for life. Though no one could say Miss Phoebe was sour – ninepence to the shilling maybe, but she had a heart under her flat chest. It was a mystery though why Salt joined their odd carry-on. She had, after all, a wedding ring on her finger, so there must have been a Mr Salt. But he was never mentioned and it was more than her life was worth to ask.

Mrs Stocks passed on the onions, neatly sliced, and went to splash cold water over her burning eyes. The pail was by the window and she could see the darkening yard and coach-house through an arched gateway.

'Aye, look there! Company already. Coach's in the yard, and land snakes, there's a nigger got down!'

'I'll have to finish the porter when I've seen to the hosses, Mrs Salt, ma'am,' said Hawkins and hurried out.

'A nigger . . . go on!' Sally was goggling with curiosity.

'Captain Meredith's nigger it'll be, and I'll thankee to get back to th'work, Sally Dade,' said Salt.

One last peer before she went back to the basting brought a gasp from Sally: 'He's coming this way!'

'The bell'll be ringing afore th'can say knife,' said Mrs Stocks. And in answer, the main bell high on the kitchen wall began to peal.

'See to the front door, Sally . . . oh save us . . . NOT with th'hands all greasy. Here use this!' and Salt threw Sally a cloth. 'Tidy th'self an'all,' she added as Sally bounced out of the kitchen.

There was a knock on the back door.

'That nigger ain't never expecting to come in *here*?' Salt

exclaimed.

'Why not?' Jess asked the question without thinking and surprised herself. Two pairs of eyes stared at her. She ploughed on: 'He goes where the Cap'n goes, and th'can't expect him to come in by the front.' She left the washing up, drying her hands on her apron, and went to open the door.

A rush of warm savoury air met Midnight. He caught a glimpse of two red faces staring at him from the depths of the kitchen behind the head of this strange boy turned girl who was forever crossing his path. He could feel reserve, even hostility, coming towards him as real as the smell of roasting meat. His own reserve increased. He stood mute.

And then Jess said: 'Come in . . . come in, afore the weather does thee an injury!' smiling at him. A free and easy smile, but lop-sided because her face was still puffy from Garty's beating. She looked so comical he was taken out of himself and stepped inside with a return of confidence.

'It's enough to freeze the arse of a cat,' Jess went on cheerfully.

'JESS!' said Salt even louder than usual. 'Th'd better soap th'tongue. And get on with th'work. The blackamoor has his master to attend to, I don't doubt.'

'I'm to wait until I'm called, ma'am,' Midnight said politely.

The eyes turned on him again.

'Hark at him!' said Mrs Stocks. 'He's as well spoken as any gent. Where did th'learn to speak like that?'

'My master taught me.'

'What – the Cap'n?'

Midnight said stiffly: 'Not my present master, the one before.'

'Who was that then?' Mrs Stocks asked, undeterred. 'Another Cap'n?'

'Mr Sanderson – of Jamaica.'

'Well I never!' Mrs Stocks put her hands on her hips. 'Jamaica. And how did he come by thee?'

'He bought me at the scramble.'

'What's a scramble?' Jess asked, though she'd noticed the questions seemed to be driving him like a snail into its shell.

'Each shipload of stolen people is brought to the merchant's yard. At a time prepared, the doors are thrown open and the slave masters run and seize as many as they can.' He moved out of the bright firelight into the shadows by the wall as if hoping to escape further questioning.

Until coming face to face with Midnight, Jess had never given much thought to slaves, and certainly had never considered them as being stolen. The new idea turned over in her mind as Mrs Stocks, all eager now, pressed for more details.

'Is that what happened to thee . . . grabbed like that? And what came after?'

Before Midnight had a chance to reply, Salt said sharply: '*He* may not have aught to do, but the rest of us haven't time to stand gossiping.' She glared and banged down the iron pan she had taken from the fire, then lifting the lid allowed a huge cloud of steam to escape into the air.

Jess felt faintly indignant at the remark. It wasn't the nigger's fault that he had nothing to do for the moment. She looked across at him. He was staring at the floor, keeping very still as if he were trying to be part of the wall. There was something mysterious about him and she wanted to ask so many questions, but he had that locked-in look, so that even if she risked Salt's caustic tongue and asked outright about how he'd come to be a slave, what it was like in Jamaica, if Africa was full of cannibals and if *he'd* eaten people, she'd probably get no more than a few shrugs for answers. It was tempting though. Perhaps . . .

But before she could form any question Sally burst in to the kitchen again, breathless; the words tumbling out:

'Wasn't only the Cap'n, there was that Dr Plumb and his missus and the sugar-baker what'sisname . . . Crayshaw *and* that Lawyer Loveitt – he's a withered customer if th'likes. Wouldn't like him to catch me under the kissing bough.'

'Th'd better mind th'words, Sally Dade. Jumped up ideas th'has. If any gent takes notice of thee it'ud be with only one thing in mind, so th'd better watch out for th'self.'

'Mrs Salt, what things th'do say! I'm a good girl.' She spluttered into her hands, staring wide-eyed over the top of her fingers.

'Take this tray of fruit and nuts through to the dining-room and try to act sensible.' Salt said, following Sally with a huge silver dish set with delicate jellies she wouldn't entrust to anyone else.

As the door closed, Mrs Stocks wiped the back of her hands over her mouth. 'I'm as dry as dust. What with the onions and the heat, every last drop of moisture's gone from me. What I could do with is a nice pint of porter!' She looked longingly at the keg, then with a casual twitch of her head, added: 'I'll see to that brandy while I'm waiting,' and slipped out to the passage and the cellar door.

'She's after a quick snort,' Jess said. 'If Mrs Salt catches her there'll be ructions.

Midnight said nothing, but edged closer to the fire.

'Cold?' she asked, guessing something of his discomfort.

'It eats me to my bones.'

'Do th'hate England so much?'

'There's not much to love.'

There wasn't, but there ought to be – Jess thought. She couldn't name many things *she* found lovable, but knew a thrill in being on the waterfront and always felt cheered by clouds racing along in the sky. Yes, the sky was lovable and was always there, no matter boxed-in the streets.

Midnight watched her from under half-closed eyelids. A white girl with African hair – untrimmed Eboe hair. He could see the huts thatched with reed; the Embrenche's day hut – his father's hut – open and filled with people. A tall woman in a loose blue calico wrap, her ankles and wrists glinting with gold in the sun, squatted on the dusty ground. Under her skilled hands a snake of clay was being coiled into the shape of a large globular jar. Quietly; certainly; it grew into faultless perfection. Now and again she wetted the clay from water into a shallow bowl, stretching and smoothing to her satisfaction with marvellous economy of movement. His mother! The rich scent of palm oil mixed with special powdered wood came to him and without knowing what he did, he sniffed his own hand.

'Is it true that white folk smell different from black folk?' Jess asked curiously.

He came back from heat and home with a jolt. 'If by that you mean are the white ones dirty, then yes.' He spoke honestly, but more harshly than he would have done if it hadn't been for the pain he carried. She didn't seem perturbed.

'Dirt's the same the world over I'd a thought.'

'But we wash it away. It is our custom to bathe in the streams near my home very often and wash always before eating. These things we do very strictly. From small children we're taught so.' He didn't understand what had persuaded him to speak so openly about his childhood.

The thought that this slave had known home and care, perhaps even love, came as a sudden shock to Jess. Something outside her experience. She said roughly:

'If th'knows so much about washing, th'd best learn summat about drying. There's a cloth hanging over the fireplace.' She pointed to the half-dry pans beside her. 'Get on with it.'

Midnight took the cloth. It was not his place to serve anyone but the Captain and if he ever found out it would mean punishment. He knew also that he hadn't the right to refuse. In some way he had offended her. Perhaps she thought he meant she smelled unpleasant to him. He took a pan, wiped it thoroughly, then took another, turning over his thoughts. If she did, then she would be the first who cared anything for his opinions since his old master died. He was curiously moved, but at the same time suspicious of his own reactions.

Jess edged towards him a fraction, sniffing; wanting to find out what her nose would tell her. But the overriding smells were of meat and pastries, and she daren't get too close. He took a handful of kitchen tools, and their eyes met.

'Are th'going to be a prizefighter after all?' Jess asked hastily. 'Cap'n's choice th'said.'

'He chooses not to choose.' he replied.

'And leaves thee adangling?' asked Tess.

'He likes to feel his power.' nodded Midnight.

'Th'should fight *him*!' Jess said. 'He needs someone to take him apart. Setting himself up as God . . . old *goat*!'

Midnight laughed, hearing his sister say: 'May a beast take you . . . a goat beast!' She was shouting after the Oye-Eboe who'd brought gunpowder, beads and dried fish to trade for wood-ash salt and the perfumed woods and earth of his tribe. Like quicksilver she was impossible to catch and ran now from his mother's restraining hand, shouting hotly because of the Oye-Eboe's sly teasing. The memory was sour-sweet, bubbling up out of the dream-past with this chance remark, as fresh and real to him as if it were happening now. It should have made him feel more imprisoned than ever, but instead brought an unexpected breath of freedom.

His laughter was well remembered. The same rich sound Jess had heard on board the brig. She still felt indignant, but the sound was too infectious and she couldn't help responding with a grin: 'It ain't funny. He's a devil. Th'should know it better than me.'

'I'm not laughing at what you say. You are right. But the saying of it cuts at the chains. So . . . I laugh.' He smiled broadly, and though she didn't really understand him, her own smile grew and she was encouraged to ask:

'What's to happen then? Will th'be sailing again with the Cap'n soon?'

He shook his head. 'Because the last voyage made no profit, *Princess* won't go to sea again until more money can be found to buy all the things needful for a fresh voyage. The syndicate aren't willing to find such money, so the Captain must wait. Perhaps *Princess* will be sold. There are rumours . . .'

But Jess was not to hear the rumours or have a chance to ask what a syndicate was, because Sally and Salt came back, and seconds later a rather rosy Mrs Stocks reappeared clutching two bottles of brandy.

'Midnight, if that's th'name, the Cap'n says th'must attend to him and the other guests in the drawing-room. Show him the way, Jess, then come straight back,' Salt instructed in a voice like hot coals.

Jess couldn't think of any words on the way up and Midnight seemed to have retreated again. He went quickly into the drawing-room, leaving her to return to the hot flurry of the kitchen.

Supper had been over a good hour and a half. The company was seated round card tables in the drawing-room, with the exception of Miss Phoebe in her usual chair and the Captain who was warming his backside at the great fire, glass in hand. There had been a good many glasses and now he signalled to Midnight who came from the shadows by the far wall, bringing a bottle of port to refill the glass held out.

'You have no taste for cards, Miss Phoebe?' The Captain formed his words with care.

'I play a little limited loo on occasion,' she answered absently, her attention on Midnight.

'No gambler myself, ma'am, Regard it as a sin. But that's my opinion and in no way . . . *no way* reflects on the present gathering.'

Midnight poured the wine. Light from the chandelier gleamed on his metal collar. Miss Phoebe noticed and pinched herself together, the tip of her tongue wetting her dry lips is if to help the words to slide out more easily, but before they came, her sister was saying loudly:

'P'raps not a gambler at the tables, but in other areas, eh, Captain?' with a wink as she looked up from her fan of cards.

'Never, ma'am!' She neighed out a laugh. 'Come now, Captain. A dabble in business. A win here . . . a loss there. Dammee man, y'lost enough of our stock!'

'You like to joke, ma'am, said the Captain reddening.
'Miss Jarman, your call,' Dr Plumb reminded her.
She turned to him sharply looking across the table: 'A minute, Doctor. In your interests . . . in all our interests. I say the Captain is a gambling man. He gambled away our . . .'

'Never gambled, ma'am. Bought and sold . . . sold, but never gambled.' He had drunk his port and now snapped his fingers for Midnight to pour another glass. 'The Middle Passage is a gamble if you like, but your gamble not mine.' He rolled his eyes upwards. 'God's will only *who* lives and dies . . . wasn't my fault some of the crew and near all those damn niggers took the flux.

Some of the wine spilled from the bottle to the floor.

'Damned Ape!' The Captain made a worse mess by inadvertently jerking the glass, then with a single gulp drank the remaining wine, turned and boxed Midnight's ear in one sequence of movements. 'Get a cloth, y'ugly devil.'

Miss Phoebe muttered something about: 'Being sure there was no need for . . .' but no one paid any attention because Sally Dade had opened the door, announcing:

'Mr Godschalk.'

'The very man.' Harriet Jarman pushed back her chair and strode between the tables, giving Midnight a quiet instruction as she passed, hand outstretched to the small man in neat brown velveret and bob wig who came in smiling timidly. She levered his arm up and down like a pump handle, then turning to the card players said: 'Bob, Joe, Mr Loveitt, Dr Plumb, ladies . . . you know Mr Godschalk from Bretyard and Pope Insurance Office.' She shepherded him towards the Captain talking all the time. '. . . not a prearranged business call, merely a social visit, eh Mr Godschalk? But there's always time for business. The Captain will have the papers on him, I'm sure – being a careful man.'

'Papers?' The Captain looked shaken.

'Bills of Sale . . . Promissory Notes from the buyers in Jamaica,' suggested Mr Godschalk.

'But I've already passed on all such things.'

'Ah, but Miss Jarman is sure there are some overlooked.'

'What are you s – suggesting?'

Mr Godschalk looked faintly dismayed. 'Nothing, I assure you. In my business, Captain Meredith, everything has to be carefully checked and checked again. The smallest hint of irregularity cannot pass unnoticed.'

The Captain jumped on the word: 'Irreg'larity. What ilreg'larity, pray?'

By now the card games were forgotten, everyone staring at the two men. Miss Jarman stood back, a slight smile on her raddled face. Aware of the interest he was causing, Mr Godschalk took his time in replying, choosing his words with care.

'A matter of a silence, Captain Meredith. On the part of Mr Lascar. You remember Mr Lascar, I'm sure. Mr *John* Lascar? Our agent in Jamaica. I would have expected a letter from him. A note at least. If we are to pay out a large sum to cover the last cargo there must be some corroboration. Didn't he give a letter to you?'

The excess of wine now seemed to have affected the Captain's movements. He lurched and grabbed at the mantelpiece to steady himself. 'It should have been with the batch of papers given. Must've. Ma'am, I appeal . . . unless . . .' He stared hard at the face of his slave who had returned with a dry cloth. 'You black bastard . . . spawn of Satan . . . this your work! Y'devious slimy way of bringing disrepute.' He took hold of Midnight's arm, cruelly digging in with his fingers. 'They said things of you out in the Indies . . . Obeah, they said. Devil-man. As a God-fearing man I took n'heed. Such things are naught but feeble threats to ig – gnor'nt peasants. But there's no smoke without fire. The evil's there, lying dorm'nt waiting ash . . . shance t'strike . . .' The Captain's words slipped and slithered as his outrageous temper blew up into

unbelievable fury, all reason washed away by wine.
'Hanging's t'good,' he added. 'I'll slice strips of y'black
skin and peel them back one by one, like a damned
banana.'

Jess, who had come in response to the message brought
by Midnight from Miss Jarman, stood in the doorway
appalled. She took in the bloated rage of the Captain, the
eager faces of the card players who were savouring every
minute, the dry Insurance man with his cool uncaring
manner, the old harridan who'd set it all in motion. They
were like a great flock of gulls swooping to tear and gobble
at their prey. Midnight. Helpless. Standing frozen. She
wanted to punch and kick them, give them some of the
treatment they doled out so carelessly. She was ready to
speak out, but Miss Jarman beckoned her over.

'Corroboration, Captain? The wench has that. Estate
in Jamaica waiting for you, bought with my money . . . *our*
money!' She spread her arms to draw in her colleagues.

I never said that – Jess thought, the ground feeling as if
it was weakening under her feet. She tried hard to think
back and remember exactly what she'd said that first night
in Jarman House. Surely nothing that definite? She'd
been so tired, so bloated and sleepy with food. Estate . . .
Kingdom? Yes, she'd repeated those same words the Cap'n
had spoken on board the brig, though she'd no notion
what he meant. And now the old baggage was twisting
everything; building something out of nothing. Was she
trying to frighten *him*? The idea was so daft she would
have laughed except for the Captain's searing glance,
which rested for no more than a second on her before
returning to burn into Midnight as he breathed:

'I'll snuff your light out, nigger . . . OUT!'

The contrast between his former colossal outburst and
those whispered words brought a cold sickening reality.

Jess felt it like a sickening blow. She was quite unprepared for Miss Phoebe's reaction. She hadn't even noticed her until now, when she stood up, trembling, words coming out in an uncharacteristic torrent.

'How can you stand there talking about bits of paper and profits and money . . . *money*,' she made the word into an excrescence, 'when what you are doing is playing with a human soul. You don't care about *people*, only about your shoddy greed. Don't you know you're using that boy like bait to catch a fish? The girl too . . . oh . . .' Suddenly she seemed to take in the reality of what she was doing and all her confidence fled. She put her hands over her face and burst into tears, scurrying towards the door. As she passed, Jess said involuntarily:

'That were grand, miss!'

Briefly Miss Phoebe hesitated, startled by the words. She brought her hands away from her face only long enough for one look before continuing into the hall and up the stairs.

The moment of warm contact waned, leaving Jess to fend for herself.

Eight

In the days following the Frolic, life dropped into a dull routine which Jess welcomed. She had fully expected to be dismissed the next morning, but nothing was said and she didn't ask. Salt kept her hard at work round the house from the time she woke till late at night, with grim satisfaction in seeing her too worn out to do more than fall into bed and sleep.

'Hard work brings its own reward,' she said more than once.

The only reward seemed to be exhaustion and Salt's sour amusement, but Jess didn't complain. Only a fool complained with a full belly. There were moments when she wondered if there wasn't more in life for her than being put to work. Particularly when she was dusting the shelves in the study. All those books. They were bursting to tell her things she would never know. If only she could read they might open up the world. The old baggages read, specially Miss Phoebe.

One morning Jess stopped dusting and took a book from the shelf, admiring the gold edges to the pages and the soft green leather binding. Inside small printed letters made a neat pattern but nothing more.

'I didn't know you could read, Jess,' Miss Phoebe said, coming in like a whisper.

Startled, Jess almost dropped the book, then hastily replaced it on the shelf. 'I can't. I were dusting, miss, naught else.' She expected to be told to get on with her work and not waste time, but instead Miss Phoebe became unusually animated.

'Reading is such a joy. In fact with me it is a passion. A passion born of the habit I came by as a girl at school. Only a dame school it was – nothing so grand as the Academy for Young Ladies Miss Hannah More keeps in Wark Street now – but our teacher, Mrs Ellis, was a *great* reader and always encouraged us children to have regular reading times. She wrote poetry too. All about the seasons and flowers and animals. What do you think of that?' and when Jess stayed quiet, she sighed, moving towards the books to touch them with loving fingers. 'She was a beautiful person . . . a Quaker . . . and had high moral ideals. I tell Harriet – er, Miss Jarman – this, but she . . . she won't . . .' The words faded and she looked about her with slightly flushed cheeks. Jess got the impression she felt a little embarrassed at having been so frank before a servant. But the temptation of a listening ear seemed to overcome her scruples and she went on more furtively:

'She's set against them you know . . . and all because they work to abolish the slave trade. Yes . . . yes indeed . . .' she was nodding and glancing at Jess, then away, the flush in her cheeks ripening. 'I wish . . . that is, I feel it is my duty . . . no, no, my *desire and* my duty to join their Society, but Miss Jarman won't countenance it.' She stopped abruptly, looked about her once more, then scuttled out, leaving Jess astonished by such confidences.

It wasn't the end of the encounter. Coming into the drawing-room later that day to bring in the tray of tea, Jess found Miss Phoebe standing by the long window. She began talking as if the conversation of the morning had been only briefly interrupted.

'The Society of Friends do such *good*. I can't imagine . . .

that is, my sister does take such a *strong* view. I don't wish
to upset her, but sometimes it is only *right* to follow one's
own convictions. It's very difficult . . . very difficult indeed
. . .' She left the window, taking small steps towards the
table.

Jess looked at the worried forehead wrinkles, the
nervous hands fussing over the teacups, plum cake and
shortbread. She thought what an undecided old fool
Phoebe was, but it made her outburst at the Frolic all the
more courageous. Unwilling admiration wrung from Jess a
kind of exasperated protectiveness, as if *she* were the
mistress and Miss Phoebe in her care. It was absurd, but
the sight of her helpless under the burden of her own
inadequacies toughened Jess's attitude towards Miss
Jarman. She was an old cow and a mean old cow at that.
Giving in to her was no answer at all.

'Sometimes I think . . .' Characteristically, Miss Phoebe's
words trailed away.

'Th'should stand firm,' Jess said, letting her new role
take over, then going very red at her own daring. She
expected to be sent out with a flea in her ear.

But Miss Phoebe said: 'You think so?'

'I do, miss!' Jess said, aghast at her own boldness.

Miss Phoebe looked at Jess, caught her eye, flushed so
deeply that the ugly pits stood out on her skin, then looked
quickly away. In that moment Miss Jarman came into the
room.

'This is not a proper conversation,' Miss Phoebe
murmured, and more loudly: 'A few slices of thin bread
and butter as well, Jess.'

'Yes, miss,' Jess said, a servant once more. But contact
had been made again, a second time. However unwillingly,
a bond had been established.

'And where's Sally?' Miss Jarman's hard voice shattered

93

the intimacy. It was Sally's task to serve all meals.

'Poorly, ma'am. Been throwing up something terrible since midday.' Jess didn't add she'd brought it on herself, being too liberal with the gin bottle after swilling strong beer with her food.

Miss Jarman grunted and dropped into her chair. 'They're still arguing today, would you believe it?' she said to Phoebe, accepting a dish of tea and making a whirlpool with her teaspoon. 'Idiots, the lot of 'em. Can't see what's in front of their noses. Told 'em at the Frolic that scurvy Captain's rooking us . . . and what's the answer? Proof, says Loveitt . . . something to stand in a Court of Law!'

'But how do you know, Harriet?' Miss Phoebe asked.

'Know? What do you mean, *know?*' Miss Jarman seemed astonished by the question.

'Know that the Captain has been . . . er . . . swindling us?' Miss Phoebe said, after a strengthening glance at Jess, whose curiosity was making her linger.

'There's no question, no question at all.'

Miss Phoebe swallowed. 'But what he said might be true . . . about the . . . er . . . slaves dying and there being no sale. Slaves *do* die in their thousands.'

Miss Jarman stared as if unable to believe her ears. 'You've let y'self be hoodwinked by that knave, though the Lord knows why! I tellee he's a swindler. That should be enough for you.'

This time Phoebe was quenched. She sat down, avoiding Jess's eyes. Miss Jarman drank noisily, put down her cup and added:

'Mark my words, this business will drag on and on. *Princess* is to stay in dock. I've seen to that. There'll be no more doubtful voyages till the thing is settled one way or another. Know what I told 'em?

Miss Phoebe gave her head a slight shake, holding on to

the arms of her chair as if it would save her from drowning.
'I said . . .'

But Jess was not to learn what she said, because Miss
Jarman suddenly realised she was still there and said
brusquely: 'What do you think you're at? Thought you
were to fetch a plate of bread and butter? Off with you.'

Jess went, returning with the plate in a few moments,
then retreating just as quickly.

It was cold in the large panelled hall, in spite of the
early breath of spring which had brought purple and gold
crocus spears into the rough grass. The kitchen was
draughty but warm and everyone would be pulled close to
the fire, enjoying a moment's rest before preparing the
evening meal. But Jess didn't want to share their company.
There were times when she felt imprisoned. The great oak
front door was a forbidden invitation. Out there were
clouds spreading free and birds doing as they pleased. The
back door was barred to her by the people she would have
to pass in the kitchen. There was only one way out. She
tiptoed across the wide polished boards, past the stuffed
bear with his arms full of walking sticks, the brass-faced
longcase clock, the dignified portrait of old Mr Jarman
with his watching eyes, and quietly opened the door,
drawing in great breaths of sharp fresh air, revelling in this
stolen freedom. She'd go in through the back. Invent
some reason to quieten old Nosy Salt.

Hurrying down the steps, across the carriageway and
more steps to a terraced walk, she ran towards the
shrubbery, which curved round a sloping lawn out of sight
of the drawing-room windows. There was a small secret
arbour tucked into thick laurels with a long bench to sit on
and a rose trellis curving overhead. She had found it a few
days earlier and feeling an immediate love for the place,
determined to find time to sit there. Now was the time.

As she sat down it seemed as if all the growing things drew round, sheltering her. It was a strange sensation. All her life had been spent surrounded by grimy bricks with hardly a green grass blade in sight. But here the sense of rightness grew strong, allowing her to be herself. Quietness settled in. A robin came to perch on the trellis, only an arm's distance away. Did they really peck moss to cover the faces of the dead? She couldn't believe this cheerful bird would have such mournful habits. The robin observed her fearlessly. She hadn't felt so pleased by anything in a long time. Living should always be like this rather than drudge and more drudge. How to make life peaceful was a new question that had come to tease her mind. In the old days she'd not had time to think about anything except how to keep out of trouble. Perhaps having time was the right beginning? And she hadn't much of that, but more than before and she *could* think as she worked. Salt could nag and scold as much as she pleased, force her to polish and scrub harder and faster, but she had no hold over her mind.

Satisfaction vanished with the snap of a twig. Jess stiffened, listening . . .

Silence. The robin had flown off, but she knew she wasn't alone.

*

For a long time Midnight crouched in the dark thicket, swimming between consciousness and fantasy. His ears were playing tricks, hearing the running feet of the white thieves, the fearful cries of his tribesmen. He shivered, not daring to move in case they noticed and dragged him out.

But what was he thinking? It had already happened! He stifled a moan. Shifted . . .

And was again in the scrub behind the round thatched huts that blazed like torches. Crackling, gushing smoke stung eyes and nose until he was forced from cover. Then they seized him, shouting in a strange tongue. Broad clumsy beasts, scabbed and dirty white, with knives that hacked and smoking pistols. One of them tossed a ball high in the air with a screech of laughter. It spun against the stars, and falling, turned into the head of his father.

'Oh God in the Sun . . . send down your burning spear to slay these monsters and save us . . . save us . . .'

But there was no punishing flame, only orange tongues consuming the huts and reaching out into the dark sky. Everywhere people were running and falling, screaming out in terror. His arms were pinned in agony by one of the beasts, but still he fought, kicking and struggling until a blow blotted out the world.

Don't think . . . don't think. It is over. Finished. Now is what matters. He'd escaped, hadn't he, and she was there. A small miracle after the endless hiding. Call to her! But why should she help? Why had he come? A single moment when she'd reminded him of his sister meant nothing . . .

But the African sun beat relentlessly down on his aching head. Cramped on the ground he tried to stretch and found his arms bound behind his back and his feet shackled in iron chains. In a panic he struggled and someone cried out. Only then did he realise they were all of them strung together. He closed his eyes feeling sick and faint. But there was to be no rest. One of the white thieves came with a whip, cutting legs, backs, faces; drawing blood; roaring at them until they understood he wanted them to stand up. It was then he saw his sister. She was unshackled and they were dragging her from the only remaining hut. As she struggled and cursed he called out and she tried to run to him. But the white beast with her laughed, letting her run, then catching her, once . . . twice . . . finally throwing her to the ground; rolling on top of her, defiling her . . .

He moaned again. Shifted again. And a twig snapped.

Jess got off the bench and parted the bushes, peering into the laurel darkness, her heart pounding and her breath coming shallow and fast.

'Who's there?'

'Jess!'

'You!' She was more angry than frightened now, seeing the nigger. What right had he to spoil everything?

He got up from his crouching position slowly, as if his body was hampered by a heavy weight, and came towards her. Jess glared at him, backing away until he was in the open. The impact of his changed appearance reached her gradually. It was the way he held his hands that killed her anger. He kept his bloated thumbs well away from his body, using his elbows to ease past the bushes.

'Lordy! Whatever happened?' Jess asked.

He was coatless and shivering. The neck of his shirt was open and the metal collar cut into his swollen throat.

'They beat me,' he said, his teeth chattering as if he had a fever.

'They? Who?'

'The Captain . . . Dando. Others!'

'But why?'

He shook his head, as if explanations were too difficult, swaying, almost collapsing on to the bench. She sat down beside him, instinctively putting her arm out to support him, but he jerked forward with a sharp gasp, and she saw the brown lines of dried blood across the back of his shirt.

'That devil,' she said. 'That bleeding bastard of a devil!

Here . . . what are th'going to do?'

'I've run away,' he said, staring at her with such intensity that she felt a rush of alarm. Surely he wasn't expecting help? The idea was like a bucket of cold water emptied over her head. Christmas! What did she think she was? Some kind of smuggler that could find him a secret cave to hole up in until the search died down? Because there would be a search. The Cap'n had been to Jarman House once . . . would be coming again more than likely. And time was slipping away. There'd be a search for her an' all in another five minutes.

'Can't be done,' she said, feeling shamed by the look of despair on his face, and worse still as he fought to bring back the blankness to cover it. 'Th'could try Mr Lambert.' She added hastily: 'And that crony of his'n. The one as wanted to make thee a prizefighter.' Too late she remembered his hands.

He said nothing and closed his eyes.

'They'll mend. Th'bist a strong un. Daresay th's been through enough to kill most souls.'

Still he didn't speak or open his eyes. She began to feel exasperated. Time was tearing along and there were the coals to fetch. What did the fool have to come here for? She'd get up and go. If Hawkins came along and found him it wouldn't be her fault.

Midnight opened his eyes and saw Jess surrounded by a fuzz of sunlight. The image shifted. He put out one throbbing hand as the picture receded.

'I'm all kinds of a fool,' Jess said, not going. 'Don't know what's come over me. Are th'going to faint? If th'expect me to help, then th'better not. I've lifted a few sacks of taters in me time, but I don't reckon to lift thee!'

He grinned then. A pale imitation of his broad white smile, but enough of himself back in to give her heart.

'What do you wish me to do?' he whispered.

Her mind grasshoppered. Hide him? The cellar! He was black enough to melt into the shadows . . . too risky with all the fetching of beer and port. Attic? Nosy Salt could find a pin between floorboards! Where then . . . where? The beautiful shine on his skin had gone. It looked powdery. He was sick. She wasn't going to take on more trouble . . . there was enough of her own. And imagine the uproar if the old cow found a man . . . a black man . . . *Cap'n's* black man, in the house! Horses were better considered. Had hay and warmth and . . . the hayloft!

'Can th'walk?' she asked.

'I've walked this far.'

'Lean on me then. That's it. We'll have to go back into the bushes, then take the tradesman's path.' And please let them be hanging on to their gossip and porter. Hawkins was in the kitchen when she left. He liked his porter, but if he'd gone back to the stable . . . Christmas!

Nothing stirred, not even the wind, a few sparrows and their own feet. They reached the top of the slope where the path curved towards the back door. Here lay the real danger. With the kitchen garden rising so steeply there was no cover. On the other hand, would it be any safer crawling past the window, crossing fingers and sending up prayers? She compromised on the kitchen garden with prayers, which seemed to be heard because they reached the stable unobserved. Inside, the two carriage horses moved in their stalls. The younger, a stocky brown cob, snickered and turned to look at them.

'If th'bist hoping for a piece of apple, then th'bist up in the clouds,' Jess said – and to Midnight: 'This way.'

He leaned more heavily on her shoulders. She could feel him shaking, the tremors running down into her arms. He still had enough of his wits to take great care not to let his hands touch her or anything else, but she sensed that he was on the edge of collapse. A fine cold sweat dampened her face and neck. What if he was to fall here, before they'd reached the loft? She quickened her pace, almost bringing about the catastrophe she feared, as she hurried him through a doorless opening into the outhouse beyond. It was filled with sacks of corn and oats that mingled their scents with hay from the loft above and the lingering fragrance of the last of the stored apples.

Jess pointed to a ladder by the far wall. 'Can th' manage to climb up?'

He nodded.

'I'll come after thee. There's plenty of hay for a bed. Th'll be safe enough till morning.' She'd noticed the freshly filled racks above the stalls and the clean swept floor. Nobody would want more hay that night.

The hay was in a great mound. She pulled and patted it into a comfortable pad and Midnight slumped down, leaning forward against his crooked legs, his hands draped over his knees. Looking down on him Jess was astonished and appalled at what she'd done. There was no way . . . no way at all she could prevent him being discovered. One night was the most he could expect to remain hidden. And when he was found they'd both be in such a heap of dung, they'd be lucky if they didn't find themselves nicked as thieves. At best she'd be back in the poorhouse while he . . . it didn't bear thinking of. For a moment she almost hated him. She kicked at the hay in a burst of frustration.

Midnight looked up. 'I never thought to be thanking a white girl,' he said.

'Don't trouble th'self.'

'There's no trouble. Only that which I bring. You didn't have to help me.'

'No I didn't – I really didn't. It shows I'm as daft as a

March hare.'

An echo of his old laughter came bubbling up. 'March hares must be strange daft creatures then, to be so helpful. I am in debt to you.'

'Go on!' Jess said, confused. 'I ain't done so much.' Hardly knowing why, she knelt beside him and put her hand on his sleeve as she had done once before. 'Th'did more for me when Garty was giving me a beating.'

'No,' he said. 'That I did for Mr Lambert,' but the rebuff was cancelled as he brushed her fingers using the back of his hand. A strange, tentative, almost accidental gesture.

Shaken by her own crazy act and the strength of his presence, real as the hay and the sacks of corn, she became very still. A vague confusing loneliness touched her. She said abruptly: 'If I don't go they'll come looking,' because it was true. But even more pressing was the need to escape from his discomforting gaze that could have been gratitude or suspicion or almost anything. She stood up. 'I'll try to bring th'summat to eat and drink, but I can't promise.'

'Thank you,' he said.

She had got to the top of the ladder before she remembered to ask: 'What did they do to th'hands?'

'Thumbscrews,' he said. 'The Captain has a rare talent with such things. He assures himself of my guilt. When that happens, God and righteousness are on his side.'

Her anger blazed for him. 'What guilt? What is it he blames thee for?'

'The threatened miscarriage of his plans.'

'But that's naught but lies, ain't it?' Jess said hotly. 'Th'should tell him so, not let him walk over thee!'

Midnight's head drooped as if the last of his energy had deserted him, and when he spoke his voice was muffled: 'You forget I am a slave. He would never listen. His mind is as fixed as the pole star.

'Th'shouldn't be so meek!' Jess said, climbing down a few rungs. 'The gallows is too good for un. If there was any justice they'd see him swinging.' She vanished below floor level. Then reappeared, red-faced and bursting. 'Which there ain't, nor never will be, I don't doubt, for such as us!' and vanished again, skipping out into the yard and across to the house before her tongue could betray her even further.

'And where's th'been, Jess Peters?' Salt was scowling at her like a dried prune.

Jess latched the door carefully before saying: 'In the garden.'

'*Garden?*' Salt looked round at an unusually pale and quiet Sally sitting by the fire. 'Hark at the huzzy!' Her glance travelled to Hawkins who was putting down his mug and standing up. 'Slippery as a dose of rhubarb. Didn't I say?'

Jess went to fetch the coal bucket, trailing the fast dying hope that if she got on with her work she might be left in peace to think things out.

'Miss Jarman told thee to take a stroll I suppose,' Salt said sarcastically.

'Miss Phoebe,' Jess said, throwing caution to the winds. '"Go out of the front and in at the back!" Her very words.' She spoke firmly, knowing it was the only way to lie.

'Well, I'll be . . .'

'She said "A breath of fresh air is worth any doctor's potion",' Jess interrupted. 'Th'd better take note, Sally. Th'looks peaky.'

'My belly wouldn't take me that far,' Sally groaned.

'It ain't th'belly th'would be walking on. Folk mostly used their legs,' Jess said tartly.

Salt stared at them. 'Not a crumb of sense to share between thee. Get the coals and look sharp.'

The crisis was over, but only for the moment. For the rest of that evening and long after she had gone to bed, Jess was torn by worry, annoyance and something she couldn't define. In the attic room she lay on the narrow straw mattress listening to Sally's snores watching stars brighten in the charcoal sky and struggling to push away the growing sense of responsibility. She'd done enough, hadn't she? Found him shelter for the night. Saved a crust of bread and a slice of the brawn from her own supper. She'd take that to him. What more was expected?

But it wasn't duty that took her from her bed creeping down the stairs. She filled a jug with water from the pail, found rag, a tankard and another crust of bread to add to the food in her pocket. Taking the lanthorn from the shelf, she lit the tallow candle-stub from the fire's dying embers, then went out into the hard brilliance of the moonlight.

Reckon there's a hole in th'head where th'brains have flown out – she thought as she sneaked into the stable with her heart fluttering in her throat. The horses moved in their stalls as she passed them and threaded her way to the ladder. She made two journeys up it, muttering to herself. 'It's the last thing I do for the nigger. The very last. He'll have to be away before sun up.'

But there would be no going anywhere. She knew as soon as she saw him. In the cold light that streamed through the small window across his face, she saw his half-open eyes, his tongue licking dry lips, and heard the quick harsh breathing. She held up the lanthorn for a better look.

'Cold.' His whole body quivered under the covering of hay.

Jess put down the lanthorn and felt his forehead. It was burning hot. The metal collar bit into his neck. She fetched the jug, and after filling the tankard, dipped a piece of rag into the remaining water and wiped his face.

'Can th'sit up?'

He struggled painfully on to one elbow, guarding his hands, and she put the tankard to his lips. He drank thirstily, spilling some of the water because he couldn't control his shudders. He said again:

'So cold,' sliding down into the hay.

Jess set the tankard down and began to unbutton his shirt.

'No!' He was trying to hold it to his chest.

'If th'wants to get well, then th'must let me tend thee,' she insisted, undoing the last button and opening his shirt. She picked up the lanthorn again to get a clearer view, and what she saw deeply etched into his right shoulder burned into her mind as hot metal had burned into his flesh. A slave's brand mark, old and healed now. She knew of the way white-hot irons were stamped on every slave, but the sight of the scar brought a prickle of real fear. For a second she felt as he must have felt waiting for the glowing metal to eat into the skin. She put the lanthorn down and made herself quietly continue to ease the sticky shirt from his body. It was glued in places by dried blood, and he flinched as she peeled it away. He rolled over and the moonlight lay on a second different brandmark – a double triangle scarring his shoulderblade – and revealed ugly inflamed ridges striping his back from waist to neck.

The anger she had felt before was a pale moth of a feeling compared with the new anger that came now. She tore a fresh piece of rag, dipped it in the water and gently began to wipe away blood and pus. Her hands obeyed her efficiently, but inside, uncontrolled waves of rage squeezed against the frame of her body until she thought she must burst.

She had done all she could – bathed the weals, wrapped

wet rags round the swollen hands, even taken off her new cotton petticoat to cover his back. She spread hay over him for warmth, but it seemed as if the fever would shake him to pieces.

'Jess . . . you must . . . go.' The words jerked out of him as he shook.

He was right, but she couldn't leave him like this. She glanced through the window in a half-hearted attempt to tell the hour. What if someone came? What if she fell asleep?

She crouched down and pinched out the light, then burrowed into the hay, pushing up against his chest. 'I'll not leave thee to freeze,' she said.

Nine

The burning midday sun roused him from a feverish sleep. How could he have been so foolish as to stretch out away from the shade of the trees? The palm wine he'd drunk at the evening banquet must have driven all sense from him . . . his first taste. He was no longer a child, but a man. How hot it was. Thinking was difficult . . . and the banquet was at night. This was day. *Must* be! There was a muddle in his head. Not the African sun . . . the sun of Jamaica. He'd overslept. There would be punishment waiting for him when he got back to the house. Gomer would be standing at the top of the steps, lounging against the porch pillars; an ogre with his two-tailed knotted whip. The Master was against whipping. Only field niggers were sometimes punished in the privacy between the sugar canes. Gomer could beat them unseen, unheard. But he was not a field nigger, he was a house slave. It was all wrong. No escape . . . no escape . . .

Midnight opened his eyes wide, unable to understand where he was. He was lying stiffly on one side and curled close to him was a girl. A white girl. Jess! The name came from out of his dreams, but he could make nothing of it. Heat consumed him. His tongue was a desert. He shifted, and an agony travelled from his back, through all his nerves, throbbing into his hands, making him groan and rock.

The movement woke the girl. She turned and looked

at him, then sat up with a gasp of dismay.

'God Almighty, I went to sleep!'

Why was she there? And where was this place? Think . . . think . . . But he couldn't. It was too hot.

'Water!' he begged in his own tongue, but she didn't seem to understand. He tried again, using the strange English word because she was white. 'Water!'

Jess scrambled to her feet and hastily poured water into the tankard; and stopped. He couldn't drink that. It was tainted from bathing his back. She'd have to get more. But it was daylight. Salt would be up – Sally too. Oh Christmas, what a mess!

'I'll bring th'some fresh,' she said, pouring it back in the jug. 'I'll try not to be long.' She picked up the lanthorn and hesitated. He looked so queer. Sort of wild. As if he'd no idea where he was. The awful thought that he might come wandering down in a daze and be seen, made her turn cold. But there was nothing she could do about it.

'If th'stays quiet, no one'll notice thee,' she said. 'I'll visit when I can.'

He didn't answer, just went on staring at her as if she was talking gibberish. Perhaps the fever had taken his wits. With a shiver she hurried to the ladder desperately hoping that Hawkins wasn't about. There was no one in the stable or the yard, but when she came close to the back door she could hear voices from the kitchen.

'Not a sign, Mrs Salt. I searched all over.' It was Sally's voice.

'What did I always say? There's no trusting a guttersnipe. Bad down to the bones. Brought up to thieve and . . . Mercy on us, the silver!'

Boldness was the only card she had. Hiding jug and lanthorn behind the water butt, Jess opened the door and walked into the kitchen.

Salt and Sally were standing by the table. Sally with her sleeves rolled up and her hands black with ashes from the dead fire. They stared at her as if she'd turned into a circus freak. For a wild moment Jess was convinced she must look different after a night spent sleeping beside the nigger. If they knew they'd never try to find out why, but would drive her out there and then. Tell her to get down to Marsh Street and join the rest of the whores. Oh, it wasn't like it seemed, but who would believe her? No going back. She'd taken the nigger's side against the world. The slave's side . . . and even Miss Phoebe would be hard put to understand. As for Salt and the rest of them, they'd goggle and gape and point at their foreheads. It'ud be worse than useless telling them she thought the Cap'n's slave had rights, needed care and attention and . . . and . . . she'd better speak out before they'd had a chance to ask awkward questions!

'Couldn't sleep. Not a wink all night did I get, so I went for a breath of air.'

'It's thy task to get up first and see to the fire. What do I find when I come down? An empty grate and cold kettle. Salt had recovered from her first surprise and was about to launch into a longer attack. Jess sighed. It was going to be a terrible morning.

'And the copper should be lit b'now,' Salt continued, getting into her stride. 'Mrs Stocks'll be here directly, and *no hot water*. A five-week pile of dirty linen and no hot water! Well don't stand like a lump of dozy puddin' – take some sticks and tinder and get started. Th'can think about what Miss Jarman'll have to say about th'habits when I tell her.'

'I ain't done nothing,' Jess protested.

''Twas thee as said it! Th'bist kitchen skivvy, not a lady who can take trips into the garden when the fancy strikes.

Good money they pays thee. Best earn it.'

Jess thought about the one and sixpence she'd had already without permission. She wouldn't feel one twitch of guilt if it wasn't for Miss Phoebe. And that was a surprise. For the first time in her life she'd allowed someone to hook on to her. She wasn't exactly fond of the old baggage. It was less clear than that, but just as relentless. The feeling bound her to the household, just as her own actions now bound her to the nigger, and the two things were tied together yet so opposite they were pulling her apart.

The wash-house sat between the stabling and a dark windowless place where coals and winter logs were stored. Squatting in front of the fire door, Jess battled with a little pyramid of dried hay and sticks she had built under the copper. She was all thumbs; sweating and grumbling. It wasn't the firemaking that had turned sour on her, it was the ravelled mesh of events and her own emotions. To have Midnight lying almost above her head and yet to be incapable of protecting him, or even taking the water he needed, was a kind of torment. Instead of being afeared for herself, she was fretting for him. She couldn't forget those brand marks. Somehow they were more terrible then the real threat of the oozing wounds across his back.

At last the fire agreed to burn. She made a hill of small coals and began to tidy up. Waiting lengthened the seconds. Waiting for the inescapable shout of discovery. Who would find him? Hawkins? Hawkins it must be.

She went back to the kitchen and found Mrs Stocks there with her daughter, Nancy. Salt was making a meal of Jess's shortcomings and Nancy stared at the new kitchen wench while her mother nodded in her easy-going way as she took off her shawl and recaptured her dropping hairpins.

Perhaps it wasn't going to be Hawkins after all. Mrs Stocks would come rushing in from the wash-house in a lather of soapsuds and thrills at having found the Cap'n's blackamoor wandering in the yard.

But predictions were destined to be wrong. The day dragged on in ordinary fashion until Jess felt she would scream. Twice she tried to get water to Midnight. The first time she got no further than filling the tankard.

'The warmer weather makes a body that dry,' Mrs Stocks commented, coming in to collect another load of dirty clothes. 'When th've had th'drink and polished off those breakfast dishes, Mrs Salt says to give me a hand.'

Jess made a pretence of drinking the water.

The second time was when she was ready to go to the wash-house. She had decided it oughtn't to be too difficult to slip into the stables and up the ladder first, but this time she didn't even reach the water pail. Salt came back from the morning-room with a self-satisfied air.

'I've spoken to Miss Jarman,' she began, and then there was a shriek from the yard and a babble of voices.

Jess abandoned all idea of water and ran out along the path and through the gateway with Salt limping behind. Nancy was standing in the middle of the yard with her hands to her face, shouting about a black bogey she'd seen at the window of the hayloft. Her mother was trying to quieten her and Hawkins was disappearing into the stables. Jess ran after him. He was climbing the ladder when she reached him, and had a pitchfork in his hand.

'Stay outside, Jess. If there's anyone up atop they might give trouble.'

Jess said desperately: Don't hurt un, Mr Hawkins.'
'I'll not start a fight if that's what's troubling thee. Get back in the yard, lass.'

Jess didn't move.

'Go on!' He was looking at her strangely.

She took a step backwards and this seemed to satisfy him, because he went on up the ladder. She heard him grunt, then call out:

'Th've no right up here. Get on th'feet.'

There was a scuffling sound then a thump, as if someone had fallen. Unable to bear the suspense, Jess tucked her skirts under one arm and clambered up to see for herself.

Midnight was lying on the floor away from the bed she had made him. His eyes were open but it was obvious he didn't know where he was. Sweat shone on his face and neck. His back was a mat of hay. Hawkins was standing at the top where he'd climbed from the ladder and was gazing nonplussed at the strange scarecrow on the floor. In the suspended moment Jess saw a long strand of cobweb stretching from window to floor, flecks of dust spinning in a shaft of sunlight, her petticoat in a ball against a pile of hay, the filthy shirt on the nail where she'd hung it the night before. She shook herself back into life and moved to step into the loft.

'Mind out! He might harm thee,' Hawkins warned, his usual mild manner gone. 'I told thee to get out into the yard.'

'There's no harm in him,' Jess said. 'He's weak as a kitten. Can't th'see he's ill?' She went close and bent over Midnight, scolding herself for ever having left him. She should have gone straight to Miss Phoebe. Explained. Begged for her help. But it was too late. Much too late.

Hawkins crouched beside her. ' "Midnight," ' he read. ' "Property of Captain Abel Meredith". Well I be blowed . . . I never recognised un!

From below Harriet Jarman's strident voice called: 'Hawkins! Are you there? Show yourself, man.'

Jess looked at him in mute hopeless appeal. He shook his head and stood up, moving to the hole in the floor so he could be seen.

'Here, ma'am!'

'What's happening up there? Nancy's having hysterics and raving about a black ghost, of all ridiculous things. No sense to be got from anyone.'

'It's the Cap'n's blackamoor, ma'am. Nothing I can't handle.

Midnight moved restlessly. A thread of spittle ran from the corner of his mouth and down his chin. His eyelids lifted. For a brief moment there was recognition in his eyes and he reached for her hand, pulling back in his eyes and he reached for her hand, pulling back before the contact was made. Coldness settled in her stomach, hearing Miss Jarman bark out:

'Dammee, I'll not have that nigger . . . any nigger on my property. Get him down here at once and show him through the gates. Spying, I don't doubt. Oh, that Captain's a crafty one.'

'It's not like that, ma'am,' Hawkins began.

'Don't argue. Bring him down. You've got a pitchfork. Use it!'

Jess whispered: 'Go down th'self. She'll not be satisfied till th'do.

'She won't listen. I knows her.'

'All right. I'll go.' She touched Midnight's shoulder and said in his ear: 'I'll not desert thee,' then stood up and went to climb down the ladder.

'You! I didn't ask for you to come down,' Miss Jarman greeted her as she reached the bottom. 'Where's that nigger?'

'He's ill,' Jess said. 'He can't move easily.'

Miss Jarman looked at her – a long calculating look that

gave Jess the shivers. When she spoke again it was slowly and with great emphasis. 'If he has to be tied in a sack and dragged, I'll have him down.'

'His soul's gone . . . he's like a dead man.' Jess exaggerated in her indignation and anxiety.

'Then he won't put up any fight. Down and out to the street where he belongs!' She adjusted the lapels of her severe jacket, stabbed another look into Jess and marched from the outhouse.

They got Midnight down in half an hour, after Jess had fetched water for him to drink, and then had cleaned him as best she could. The activity seemed to rouse him from his stupor. He spoke to her twice in his own language and then said: 'I am stupid . . . the fever . . .'

'Don't talk,' Jess said. Save th'strength to get down the ladder.'

He forced himself on to hands and knees, obeying like a dog, without question. Trusting her. And that was a relief and a horror together.

'Th'best go down first and catch his legs when I've helped him on to the ladder,' Jess told Hawkins. 'I'll come after.'

They brought him into the yard lolling between them like a rag doll – arms draped over their shoulders. Miss Jarman took one look, then said: 'In the kitchen.'

Miss Phoebe was hovering in the background. Jess looked at her as she passed, questioning without words. Asking for support. But Phoebe looked away. No help there. Jess felt such a deep sense of disappointment that she was startled by it. She barely glanced at the other women who clustered round staring, washing forgotten in the excitement of this unexpected entertainment.

After they had lowered Midnight on to a chair and propped his arms on the table in front, Hawkins stood back, but Jess stayed close. She put her hand defiantly on his arm and glared at the ring of faces. She could feel him trembling with fever and cold, although he was close to the fire which burned merrily now. There was a silence. Then Harriet spoke, but not to Midnight.

'You seem to have knowledge of this, Jess Peters. Start at the beginning.'

'I don't know any beginning,' Jess said. 'Only that he were hiding in the garden.'

'Didn't I tell thee . . . didn't I say!' Salt couldn't contain her triumph. 'Twice she's been roaming the garden. Yesterday and again this morning early, ma'am.

'That so?'

'I never denied it,' Jess said truculently.'

'How did he get in that state?'

'Cap'n Meredith beat him . . . Cap'n and some others.'

'Why?'

'I don't know no more, except that I helped him to hide in the hayloft. He was running away – not that he had any need. He's a free man.' Jess spoke fiercely, not taking her eyes from the raddled face, daring her to deny it.

'Poppycock! There's laws and laws as you seem not to know.' Harriet Jarman was speaking to Jess but looking at her sister, who was standing a little apart as if she wanted to fade into the wall behind.

Jess made a last appeal. 'Say it's true, Miss Phoebe. It must be true. I heard Mr Loveitt say summat like it with his own lips, and the landlord down at the Seven Stars.' It was immensely important to have the old baggage side with her.

'Slave-holding in England is against the law. Case of the Negro Sommersett seventeen seventy-two,' Miss Phoebe murmured as if repeating a lesson.

'Of course. We all know that.' Harriet said roughly.

'But there's a big gap between the letter of the law and fact. *He's* a fact.' She pointed at Midnight. 'Captain Meredith's a fact. And the fact that he bought the blackamoor and is as mean and pinching and sly as a ferret, is the biggest fact of all. But I'll beat him yet. At his own game I'll beat him!' She leaned on the table – her head jutting forward, wisps of iron-grey hair sticking from beneath the cap which she had not yet changed for a wig – and asked Midnight: 'What do y'know of the Captain's affairs? A good deal, I don't doubt. Tell me!'

Midnight raised his head with difficulty. He tried to form words and then coughed. The effort made him flop forwards on to the table.

'Come on . . . speak out! I will have an answer!'

All the simmering anger in Jess flared up. She forgot about her own precarious position, her fears of being thrown out, of being caught again by Samson or Garty. This time she couldn't stand by and meekly witness cruelty.

'Can't th'see he ain't able to talk? And if he could, why should he help thee? Naught's happened as 'ud make him want to help any white folk.' Gone was her 'place' now, her hope of earning a 'character'. There was nothing left but the waiting streets. Might as well hang for a sheep as a lamb. 'Besides, he's a right to some help. He's human like the rest of us.' She looked across at Miss Phoebe, willing her to make a stand, but the surprise came from Harriet.

'See he has a bed and care. He can lay in your quarters over the stable, Hawkins. Jess Peters can help with the nursing. I want him cured. No dying . . . nothing like that.'

Jess gaped, struggling to understand. 'Th'want me to stay?'

'Naturally.'

They were all staring, even Miss Phoebe. Looking at them, Jess knew they were as dumfounded as she was. She tried again:

'I'm not to be turned into the street?'

Harriet Jarman clicked tongue against teeth with impatience. 'No indeed! Nor the blackamoor neither. Not while the Captain and I are at war. And if y'don't understand then you're duller than I thought.' With nor more than a curt nod and a: 'Come Phoebe!' she hooked her arm through her sister's and swept her from the kitchen.

The subdued murmurs swelled into gossiping chatter and half-indignant laughter. Jess scarcely heard. The news of her temporary reprieve was bitter-sweet.

'Us and them,' she said under her breath. 'No exceptions,' remembering Miss Phoebe's protest with depressing pain and no sympathy at all for herself. She should've known . . . *had* known. But she'd still let herself be fool enough to cling to the wisp of hope there might be someone of position who saw things different. Who'd stand firm. Instead she and Midnight were to be housed and fed to suit an old woman's cracked-brain scheme. They weren't people, they were bait!

It was Mrs Stocks who brought Jess out of her uncomfortable thoughts, saying:

'Poor beggar! Did thee ever see such a mess? Get some salt water for his back, Jess. A dose of Peruvian Bark for the fever wouldn't come amiss. There's half a bottle left over from that whirligigousticon sickness last winter. I've seen it on the pantry shelf, Mrs Salt. Shall I fetch it?

Ten

There were two rooms above the stable and adjacent to the hayloft. Hawkins and Jess took the slave to the one which housed the old pony tack, the moth-eaten horse blankets, the bits and pieces from Mr Jarman's horse-riding lifetime and his father's before him.

'I ain't going to share my room – not for a peck o'corn! After all a man's got a right to a place of his own.'

He means himself – Jess thought, reading Hawkins's stubborn expression – but the nigger's got just as much right! She drew a blanket over Midnight, who was lying huddled on the floor, and went to get straw for a bed. He shivered ceaselessly, eyes half closed, and from time to time swallowed with difficulty, trying to ease the collar around his neck.

'Ain't there some way we can get un off?' Jess asked Hawkins. 'Miss Jarman ain't going to like it if he chokes,' but she was thinking only of Midnight.

'No key.' Hawkins bent over the slave and examined the padlock. 'It weren't made to open easily.'

'Can't we break un with a hammer?'

Midnight moved restlessly, muttering in words they couldn't understand.

'Too close to his head. Besides he's out of his wits. He'd never lie still enough . . . not even to file it, and that 'ud be a long business.'

'Oh he would . . . he would.' Suddenly it seemed all

important to get rid of the terrible thing. 'Have th'got a file as 'ud do the task?' There was one in Samson's smithy, but that was as far out of reach as Africa.

Hawkins hesitated. 'I dunno . . . there is one, but . . .'

'Go on, Mr Hawkins, get it do. There's naught like trying,' she pleaded. 'I'll finish his bed and get him to lie on his side to make it easy for thee. He'll help all he can – you see.'

'It'll take all night to cut through a padlock like that!' Hawkins protested, but he went out of the room.

He was right. The collar didn't come off until the following day. They didn't stay up all night, but took turns working any movement they could spare, hampered by Midnight's lapses into delirium when he twisted and thrashed, making the job impossible. It was Jess who finally cut through. She had come in with fresh water to bathe his back and hands, and stole extra time to finish the job, because he was conscious and willing to lie still.

'Done it!' She was triumphant, and slid the padlock out of the iron loops, intending to take off the collar, but Midnight said:

'I will do it.'

With his hands so painful, the effort of holding open the springy collar enough to slide it from round his neck made him sweat. He dropped it to the floor and Jess kicked it out of the way. He didn't speak, but there was no mistaking his smile of pure joy. The happiness of it wrapped round and included her. She wanted to leap about, *do* something to express how she felt, sharing his delight. But he had closed his eyes, breathing fast and shallow under the fever. Crouching down in order to finish dressing his back afresh, she was surprised to feel a lump come into her throat and saw him through sudden tears, making her confused and uneasy. What should have been a great event was diminished.

The uneasiness grew as days and weeks passed. Midnight's suppurating wounds gradually cleaned, but the intense sickness only slowly subsided, giving way to a low fever that sapped his strength and depressed his mind. As if that wasn't enough, the kitchen was full of gossip about Captain Meredith being so enraged by the loss of his nigger, he was like a man demented.

'*Demented* I tellee,' Sally Dade said, revelling in this juicy bit of news that brought her so much attention. 'It's as true as I stand here . . . had it from Mary Daniels as works at the Galleon. He was near foaming at the mouth she said.'

'Oh, nonsense!' Salt was unable to take this exaggeration.

'Th'can ask her then,' Sally said, in a huff at being doubted. 'Foaming! And his face like a ripe damson.'

Jess listened but didn't take part although she could believe what was said. The knot in her stomach tightened as she wondered how long it would be before the Cap'n discovered where Midnight was hiding. She looked at Sally. A few coppers would be enough to loosen *her* tongue. She slipped out of the kitchen and hurried across to the stables to warn her friend.

But the weeks lengthened without discovery. May slid into June and Midnight was still Miss Jarman's prisoner.

It ain't right – Hawkins thought – keeping a nigger locked up here like this. It ain't decent. Being gaffer's gone to her head. It's ill-fitting in a woman. He shook his own head sadly, regretting past days, looking down at the limp form of Midnight sleeping stretched out on his stomach on the patched-up bed of hay and horse blankets. Early morning summer light came through the barred window and lay on his uncovered back, making a chequered pattern with his freshly healed wounds. The flesh had mended, but a persistent weakening fever had come back again and again. Hawkins shook his head a second time and went out to start the day's work.

The creak and click of door and padlock roused Midnight. He yawned and turned over, forgetting. The blanket rubbed his tender back, setting up a prickle of pain. Deliberately he settled flat, inviting the pain to do its worst; quietly enjoying conquering it and himself. But the sight and sound of the cramped black hole of the slave ship flashed into the forefront of his mind, as it did every day. Hot flesh pressed close; the septic flesh of his companions. On the shelf below him the old man was vomiting again, too weak even to roll over so that blood and mucus oozed down his chin and neck, some of it bubbling back into his throat. The sound of choking woke the boy next to him out of dreams of home, shocking him into knowing the hideous rocking hole where they lay. He closed his eyes and bayed in anguish. Other howls broke out. Irresistible, compelling howls. All that was left of human expression.

In the stable room Midnight heard the sound rising in his own throat. He fought to hold it down, getting up and pacing about, counting strides aloud in the English tongue, forcing himself to observe minutely every crack and cobweb, every light pattern and shadow texture over the rough brick walls and polished leather of memory. Then, almost calm, pressed his forehead against the iron bars of his prison. The window looked out on to the cobbled yard. The man Hawkins was below, moving between yard and stable. And coming through the arched gateway – Jess! Bringing him food as she had done every day of his imprisonment. He gripped the bars, wanting and not wanting to tear them down; escape; be free. But there would be no freedom. Never again. Unless he could make reality out of his dream. That needed time. So he allowed the strange old Englishwoman to play her game of gaoler. At least he was warm, dry, fed, given time. Time to think. And there was Jess.

He smiled. Then hearing the padlock rattle, hurried to lie down on the makeshift bed again. Part of his plan was not to reveal that his strength had come back, not even to Jess.

She came in carrying a bowl of porridge. He watched her from under his lashes, pretending sleep while the last rags of memory dropped away. She was the one constant thing in the past weeks of the fever that had swirled round him like a parching desert duststorm. In it faces had come close, merged, receded, disappeared. But always one face remained the same. Thin and white; large anxious green eyes; a bush of black hair. He watched her set the bowl on an upturned box. Her movements were quick but steady. There was a contenting assurance about her that he found restful. He didn't want to interrupt his own lazy pleasure in secretly observing her, by talking. She had turned and was standing, looking down on him. What was going on in her head? What did she think of him? He deliberately deepened his breathing, acutely aware of her body. It was small and skinny, with breasts that scarcely shaped the body of her dress – nothing like the tall comely women of his tribe. A strong sense of taboo made him swerve away from the direction his thoughts were taking. Just as quickly came the deep bitter distrust of all white people.

But the wish to make fun and see her laugh – laugh with her – was too tempting. He waited with eyes properly closed until he felt her breath on his cheek, her hand touch his forehead, then clapped his own over it, at the same time opening his eyes wide, smiling as she jumped.

'Oh!' She tugged at her hand, but he wouldn't let go. Abruptly she paused. Th'bist lying on th'back!'

He nodded.

'Then it's truly mended and ain't sore no more?'

He shook his head.

She stared, then said impatiently: 'Th've got no more sense than my left shoe! Say summat instead of lying there like a great mawker.'

He burst out laughing at this strange expression, then said: 'The days are hot, but at night stars as big as sovereigns make silver holes in the sky.'

Was he rambling, Jess wondered? He looked better, but he'd been in and out of his wits so many times in the past weeks there was no knowing. What was all that about stars?

'Talk sense,' she said. 'If th'can.'

'That is sense. At home the bowl of the sky is just like that. I'd like you to know how it is.'

Over the weeks of tending his back, washing and feeding him, even helping him with his most intimate needs when he was too weak to help himself and Hawkins wasn't there, she'd grown familiar with his body. But this was the first time he'd offered to share any of his inner self. She sat on the edge of his bedding, leaving her hand where it was, the physical contact suddenly taking on a new meaning.

'Tell me more. What's it like where th'come from?'

Her evident eagerness pleased him and some of the depressing mistrust was dispelled. He felt her hand warm and relaxed under his own, and said: 'There is a valley with a stream running through. Trees climb the hillside. Trees that bear plantain fruit and nuts. There are yams and eddoes and Indian corn to eat. Fish and game and

123

pineapples . . . a wealth of eating. In a clearing on a flatter piece of land is my village. My father's ground is in the middle with a wall of baked mud round it. Inside the wall are our huts. Day huts, sleeping huts. I sleep with my father and brother. My sister sleeps with my mother. Our family have the biggest huts in the village because my father is the Embrenche . . . the chief.' The telling recalled with violent clarity horrors he wanted to forget. He stopped speaking.

'Go on,' Jess said, aware of something she didn't understand.

When he took his hand away still saying nothing, she felt slightly hurt and resentful. The closeness had somehow died, but apart from this she'd been so sure there was much he could tell her. He'd travelled half round the world, seen and done things she could only guess at, while she'd never been further than Kingswood when she'd been taken to be viewed as apprentice to a nailmaker. That had been a great adventure, but it was nothing to his travels. It would be easy enough to envy him if she hadn't seen that terrible mark on his shoulder – ⒿⓈ – he'd taught her to read those letters.

He *must* teach her other things. He *must* have tales to tell. Things he'd seen on ships and in Jamaica. Anything was better than dwelling on whatever was in his mind now.

'Tell me about Jamaica then,' she said. 'I want to know what it's like . . . what th'had to do every day. Th'said th'was a house slave.'

He looked past her, his expression withdrawn and distant in the way she disliked, and when he spoke it was without warmth: 'I was personal slave to the Master and as such did personal tasks.'

'JS – was that th'master? Tell us what th'had to do for un, exactly. I ain't being gossipy. I'd like to learn all about thee . . . learn about everything!' She spread her arms wide with longing. 'Th'must know so much.'

The intense way she spoke touched him. He said mockingly: 'A slave turned teacher?'

She recognised the mockery, but didn't care. 'Th'can read and've seen so many places and folk. Not like me.' She looked at him earnestly, wanting to re-establish understanding between them. 'There ain't no one else I can talk to like this. I ain't never had a friend afore.'

He looked at her and was quiet. Jess felt embarrassed under his steady gaze. At first she could meet his eyes, but what she saw confused her and she looked at the floor, colour creeping into her cheeks, reacting against the tenderness surprised in herself with a sense of shock that made her brusque and suspicious. Where'd all her common sense gone? All the careful protection she'd built over the years. They'd gone flying out of the door leaving her wide open to any sort of hurt. Folk said only trust foreigners as far as th'could see 'em – no further. Midnight was as foreign as anyone could be. Was he not to be trusted? She didn't want that. She wanted . . .

Not knowing what she wanted, she said hurriedly: 'Eat th'porridge and put some fat on th'ribs. They're sticking out like the prongs of a garden fork. Th'looks clammed.'

'Clammed? What does that mean?'

'Starved.'

He put his hands behind his head, contemplating her. 'We shall teach each other. To start, I tell you the work of a house slave. It is to attend to all his master's needs. Clean his boots, run errands, lay out his clothes, prepare hot water for him to shave, serve the dishes of tea and coffee and the table dishes of food. But it isn't customary to stand any dish of porridge on a table out of reach.' He grinned broadly, leaving her in no doubt that she was being teased.

'Oh!' she said, glad of the diversion, and pulling a handful of hay from the bed, dropped it on his face.

With one hand he removed the hay and with the other held her shoulder, then tried stuffing the wisps down the front of her lace bodice. She pushed him away, but she was laughing in relief, and he responded by taking a firmer hold, laughing with her, briefly forgetting the soreness of his back and the tortures in his mind. She tumbled forward against him and her hair, escaping from the ribbon at the nape of her neck, made a tent for their faces. Laughter vanished. She felt his breathing quicken and the beat of his heart. His cheek was close to her mouth and impulsively she kissed it, pulling away before the fierce hunger for affection should overwhelm her altogether. She was aware that his hands had moved to her waist, then fallen back as she stood up. In a panic she ran to the door and out, forgetting to close and padlock it. She remembered halfway down the rickety ladder stairs, but for the life of her couldn't have gone back and locked him in. That would have been a final indignity. If he ran off she'd understand. There was an ache in her heart at that thought, but she didn't dare examine her feelings properly and rushed out into the yard, almost knocking into Miss Phoebe.

'Mercy on us, Jess How you do dart about. You look quite out of sorts. Is anything the matter?'

'No miss!' Jess gulped and tried to pull herself together. She was afraid the old baggage was going to start asking questions, but she didn't, and stood hesitating in her usual manner, finally asking timidly:

'The blackamoor . . . is he recovered?'

'His back's healed and the fever's gone, miss, though he's still not himself,' Jess said, wishing she could get back to her work and the oblivion of the kitchen.

'Is he . . . er . . . can he walk?

'I daresay, miss. If he had to.' Curiosity egged her on to add: 'Why d'thee ask?'

Miss Phoebe seemed not to notice this slight impudence. 'I had to inquire . . . to reassure . . .' Faint appeal touched her expression as if she was asking for help.

Jess resisted, primly folding her hands, looking down and waiting in a resigned-servant manner for permission to go. Thinking it had taken the old baggage long enough to show some concern, and it would take more than a few mumbled words to alter things.

Miss Phoebe put out a dry claw and touched Jess's arm. 'Harriet – Miss Jarman – has taken it into her head to pursue this matter against the Captain. I'd thought . . . hoped . . . that after all these weeks . . .' She dropped into agitated silence.

Jess felt a return of the old exasperation that was all wrapped up with protectiveness. She gave up trying to keep her distance.

'No good wishing that. She ain't going to let herself be defeated, not while she's got a card like Midnight to play.' To her annoyance she felt the colour flame into her face, having to say his name.

Miss Phoebe gave a sad little laugh. 'It would seem you understand her better than I do, Jess. You put me to shame. I should have done more. Thinking! It can be a curse – do you know that?' She looked at Jess, who was clearly puzzled. 'I'm rambling on . . . take no notice.' She gave herself a little shake. 'You and the blackamoor are to take a ride to Mr Loveitt's house. There is to be a meeting. Some kind of decision.' She paused as if gathering her courage. 'If the blackamoor was dying, she'd make him go. She can be . . . very hard. We . . . don't agree on such things. I had to make sure there would be no . . . hardship.'

Already weak and exposed where Midnight was concerned, this unexpected consideration broke down the last of the barriers Jess had constructed against the old woman. She had a stupid desire to cry. Miss Phoebe went on huskily:

'I've not always shown . . . thought. But it was not for want of feeling or . . . principles.' As if this confession had turned her inside out, she scurried away from Jess round the side of the house.

Surprises everywhere – Jess thought, retying her hair, smoothing her dress and trying to bring order to the thoughts that flew about in her head like dry leaves in a wind. If only there were more time to think. Time to weigh up her feelings. But she'd reached the kitchen door. There was no time . . . no time at all.

Eleven

Jess was still trying to order her thoughts as the carriage bowled down Park Street and turned into Frog Lane on the afternoon of that same day. Seated beside Miss Jarman on the faded red-leather seat, she could see houses and shops and people passing the window, and a certain pleasure added to her nervous apprehension. It was the first time she had been into the city since that awful night of the cockfight back in February. She wished there was a window in front, so she could see Midnight sitting up on the driver's seat beside Hawkins. Better still, have him inside. Perhaps then she'd learn how he felt. They'd exchanged one brief glance only since she'd run from the stable that morning. The glance had told her nothing except that he had retreated into himself again. She'd acted like a silly hen. All fussy and bothered! But if she'd stayed? The sensation that ran through her body into her limbs weakened and scared her. She fixed her eyes on the street in an attempt to calm herself.

The horses were slowing down. Hawkins called to them:

'Whoa, me lovers . . . whoa . . .' bringing the carriage to a halt outside a dignified cream-painted house – Mr Loveitt's office and chambers combined. Inside was a contrast to the bright exterior. Dark panelling; tall glass-fronted bookcases full of great leather bound books; solid brown furniture; shabby plush chairs; shabbier plush curtains hanging at high sash windows, and several very new watercolours of sailing vessels in gilt frames which looked uncomfortably out of place on the sombre walls.

Mr Loveitt was sitting behind an elegant mahogany desk. He rose as Miss Jarman and Jess were shown in, shook Miss Jarman's hand, said: 'Ah, the evidence!' eyeing Jess and: 'The other evidence?'

'In the hall,' said Miss Jarman. 'Been ill for weeks. No knowing what diseases these niggers carry about with 'em.'

Like bundles of dirty old clothes – Jess thought irritably, and looked round to see who else was there. She recognised all the people she'd seen at the dinner table in the Llandogger Trow and at the Frolic. The man with the face like Punch, the sugar-baker Bob Crayshaw, Dr Plumb and one other . . . Mr Lambert! He looked up at the mention of a nigger and was now eyeing her, as if raking through his memory.

'Sit down, ma'am . . . that's it, take the wing chair.' Mr Loveitt ignored Jess who remained were she was by the wall. 'A nip of port wine I think. Yes, yes . . .' fussing and fidgeting until everyone except Jess was supplied with a glass. 'To business! Gentlemen, you all know Miss Jarman's views about the unfortunate voyage of the *Princess*. She feels there is enough evidence now to take Captain Meredith to court. Candidly, I have my doubts. But we must examine the facts dispassionately.' He gave Miss Jarman a sideways look which Jess saw with a little skip of interest, thinking – he's got her measure; she won't fool him. For the first time she recognised that secretly she had been looking for some way out for herself and Midnight. It was obvious the lawyer thought of the scheme as being no more than one of the old cow's plaguy whims. If he'd been convinced, he would've been the first to nab the Cap'n. She felt pleased – not wanting to have anything to do with the squabbles of these upper-class money-grubbers. She and Midnight ought to run off together.

The idea came clear and brilliant!

Lawyer Loveitt had his head stuffed full of facts and he'd said all men were free in England. But free or not, no one should stop her going off with Midnight anywhere. He was the first person who'd really bothered about her. Not once had he tried to take advantage of her and now he'd had the chance. The memory of that morning flooded in, making her cringe inside. She'd not act so silly again. She'd be firm and not shamed. There was nothing shameful in making bold plans. They must go . . . they must! Not stay and wait to be thrown out after they'd ceased to be any use to the old baggage. They needn't starve. There was the prizefighting for Midnight and she could work. That Mr Randall was a sharp one and he'd tried that hard to set up a fight. He must still be interested. Or they could join the fair folk.

Buoyed up by this dazzling stream of thought, Jess didn't hear the question put to her.

'Wake up, girl!' Mr Loveitt wants to hear what you have to tell about being aboard the *Princess*.'

Miss Jarman's rasping voice cut through Jess's picture of herself as a fairground tumbler and she repeated her story in a flat monotone, conscious of a depressing conviction that the more often she told it, the more tangled she was becoming in this battle that was all about other people's money and the injured pride.

'You have a question, Mr Lambert?' Mr Loveitt said as Jess finished talking.

'It was a lad that sneaked on board. You're a girl. But there's something familiar . . . I'm not sure . . .' His bewilderment was almost comic.

131

Jess was startled. She'd been so busy with her own thoughts she'd forgotten that side of things. She said: 'That's right, sir,' because she couldn't think of anything else.

He was still floundering: 'Why were you masquerading?'

She didn't know what masquerading meant and muttered: 'Folk has to wear summat. I didn't have nothing else,' which was true, though not all the truth. He was laughing now. At her. Well let him. She didn't care.

'It's no laughing matter.' Miss Jarman snapped. 'You could do better by telling what you know. I presume you know something relevant, else why did you agree to come?'

'The Indies side of things, perhaps,' Dr Plumb suggested in the following pause while he tapped snuff on to the back of his hand, sniffed delicately with each nostril and sneezed hugely.

'I was invited,' James Lambert was deliberately distant; all his laughter wiped away. He looked acutely uncomfortable and glanced accusingly at the lawyer, who said:

'You can speak freely, I assure you. It's all in confidence.'

'You swear it? Swear I shan't have to make a court declaration?'

'Very unlikely.' Mr Loveitt played with the stem of his wine glass avoiding any chance meeting of their eyes.

'You've changed your tune, sir. It was "definitely not" when last we spoke.' James stood up. 'I'll bid you good-day. The risk is too great.'

From his seat by the window Bob Crayshaw asked anxiously: 'What's this all about risk? Risk to whom? You have knowledge of something that might bring danger?

That Captain's a mighty unscrupulous man. I've been hearing rumours about his methods of taming his crew . . . things to make your hair stand on end. I've said all along we were playing with fire.' He was becoming more and more agitated.

'You're as spineless as an up-turned jellyfish, Bob Crayshaw!' Miss Jarman's words dropped like a stone in a pond, causing ripples of protest all over the room. She was not deterred. 'Crew indeed! He wouldn't dare lay a finger on any of us. The man's a fleecer who shan't get away with it, and you . . .' she pointed a yellow finger at James, 'have a duty to inform on him.'

'I've a duty to my skin,' James Lambert said tightly.

'Which'll be flayed if you walk out on us now. I know about your debts, Mr Lambert. There are a number of people who would be only too glad to learn you have lodgings at fifteen Host Street. Newgate is a sorry hole I hear.'

There was a stunned silence.

The lawyer murmured at last: 'Let's not be hasty. Sit down, Mr Lambert, for a moment at least . . . no threats; nothing like that.'

Watching, Jess was reminded of a pack of alley cats she'd seen at the rear of Samson's smithy one night. Padding round, suspicious and edgy, waiting to spring, fight, shred each other. Only the cats had a better reason! Even cool Joe Spriggs, sitting there stroking nose and chin to a point, was as thirsty for scandal as anyone else.

'You! Fetch the blackamoor!' Mr Loveitt ordered suddenly.

Jess went out, closing the door, determined to get at least a moment of privacy. Midnight was squatting down, back against the wall, as still as the carved bear's head hanging above him. He had his eyes shut. The shabby coat that had once been old Mr Jarman's strained across his broad shoulders, the short sleeves exposing a good length of arm; the hands looking bigger than ever. She admired his hands, seeing the slender curled fingers and pink palms as if for the first time. His attitude was childlike and brought out the full force of her anger against the vultures waiting beyond the door. Hadn't he suffered enough? They'd not spare him. If he stayed silent, Miss Hugh and Mighty Jarman would make his life hell until he told all he knew. And when he did, the Cap'n would . . . She shuddered, thinking of the new puckered scars he already bore, criss-crossing with the traces of older wounds. Whatever he did would be against him.

Midnight opened his eyes, catching her unawares before she could put away her feelings. She said hurriedly: 'They want thee in there,' jerking her head towards the door.

He got up, but instead of doing as he was told, came a step nearer. 'You know what they require.' A statement rather than a question.

'I think so.' She felt weak under his gaze which was saying so much more than his words. 'Th've to tell what th'knows about the voyage.'

'And if I do – you know what that means?'

Chilled though she was by the bleakness of his voice, it was not enough to damp down the new life in her head. The pictures had to be shared, but there wasn't enough time now. She whispered:

'After . . . we'll talk then. I've things to tell thee, but not now,' pushing him through the doorway. Coming in behind him, she didn't see Midnight's glance flicker to James Lambert, then away, as if a question had been asked and answered. Miss Jarman was glaring at him with impatient curiosity and strong distaste. That too went unnoticed, but not the threat when she spoke.

'You've been brought here to give a full account of Captain Meredith's dealings. You're his slave. You were with him on board the *Princess* and before in Jamaica. Every detail, understand. That's what we mean to have – every last detail. You've reason to be grateful to me. Now's the time to show gratitude.'

Anger uncurled in Jess. She looked to see how Midnight was reacting. He showed no fear or indignation. Nothing. A little of her anger extended to him. He was as bad as Miss Phoebe. A doormat for that bullying old harridan to wipe her feet on.

Mr Loveitt intervened with practical skill: 'Excuse me, ma'am,' and to Midnight: 'It must be established first how you came to be the property of Captain Meredith. Tell us, please.'

'I was sold to him. When one master tires of a slave, it is commonplace to sell him to another.'

'And where did this take place?'

'Not until he reached the Indies. I know nothing of his voyage through the Middle Passage.' He glanced at James Lambert.

'He bought you, perhaps, after the sale of his cargo had been completed.'

'Before.'

'Before?'

'Excuse me, sir. I should say "apart". The men and women and children he had brought to be sold as slaves were a transaction quite separate from buying me.'

'I see. And how many slaves did he sell in Spanish town?'

'Forty, sir.'

'I see.' Mr Loveitt checked with the papers lying on his desk, allowing the small task to take longer than necessary, before asking sharply: 'If you know that, then you must

135

have been there. Were you sold in the same scramble?'

'No, sir. He bought me a while before.'

'Dammee, can't we get on to some real facts? All this twaddle about when this fellow was bought and sold. He must know where the money's hidden. I'll have it out of him or turn him over to the press gang. I haven't housed him for nothing. These unimportant trivialities are no more than the girl prised out of him.'

She'd do anything – Jess thought, going cold – lies out of truth. She's barmy. And Midnight? He was showing no sign of having noticed. Lordy, if he was to think she'd baited him! The old bag was still gouging like a ham-fisted butcher – face like a turkey-cock.

'Well? Out with it . . . out with it!'

Dr Plumb and Bob Crayshaw said simultaneously:

'I think Mr Loveitt can best . . .'

'This is impossible . . . uncivilised . . .'

They might not have existed for all the notice Miss Jarman took. 'Who did he deal with? What were the terms? Who else was in on it with him? Her knuckles whitened on the arms of her chair. 'I won't be put off. Won't be made an Aunt Sally for that . . . that . . . *man*!'

'You wish me to speak of plotting and bribes; banker's notes gone astray; guineas sliding into the wrong pockets?' Midnight's voice was infinitely respectful, but Jess detected a tinge of mockery and was cheered. After all he was going to fight! Make fools of 'em.

'Go on . . . go on . . .'

The old loony was hooked. Didn't she know she was being played like a fish? Jess scanned the room. None of them knew for sure – except James Lambert. There was summat wrong with him. He looked scared to death.

'There was evil done,' Midnight continued. 'Floggings, murder . . .'

'*Murder?*' Harriet Jarman seized the word.

'Is it not murder when slaves not yet dead are thrown to the sharks?' Midnight asked innocently. 'Or are driven to hang themselves from fear and despair? I myself saw a girl hang herself with a vine.'

There was a thick silence. An ugly purple flush rose up Miss Jarman's already heated face as she slowly realised how he had manipulated her questioning. In a choked voice she said:

'He's sly enough for a Quaker or that newfangled Methody. Put him in the pulpit of the New Room! Mr Wesley'd be proud of him.'

After one alarmed glance at her apoplectic face, Mr Loveitt said smoothly: 'I think we should get back to the facts. Now . . .'

She cut him short. 'Facts! The fact is, slavery is the backbone of Bristol. You all think I'm an old fool, don'tee! A woman has no business tampering with men's affairs, making a spectacle of herself because she's not got the sense to keep quiet and listen to her solid respectable betters. I can see it in your faces.' She glared round the room, daring them to contradict her and when they didn't went on: 'Take that slavery away. Allow it to be *eaten* away by fraud, and what will there be? Poverty, Ignominy.'

It was Bob Crayshaw who said peevishly: Trade's been on the downward path since the war with America. Peace don't seem to have made much difference.'

She shrivelled him with one glance. 'We can do without the American colonies. We were great before. We'll be great again. We don't need 'em. But we do need the slave trade if we're not to go under. *And I will not be hindered by slaves nor any dunderhead men!*'

And that's telling 'em – Jess thought, wanting to cheer and boo at the same time. It was all wrong and back to front, but no one could say the old baggage lacked for courage. It was better than a cockfight, and even better than the Battle.

It was obvious no one reacted the same way. Angry conversation broke out. A disturbed wasp's nest of words flying about, until the cool voice of Joe Spriggs cut through.

'Idle recriminations and sweeping statements are a waste of time. Where's the reason in pursuing something that doesn't exist? Threats haven't moved Mr Lambert or the blackamoor. We've one course left open. Put such facts as we have before the Sheriff and the Merchant Venturers and let them sort it out.'

No one was sure whether he had deliberately set a trap, or whether it was merely a chance remark that brought about such astounding results. They saw James Lambert push himself to his feet, heard his voice strained and husky say:

'For God's sake! Montserrat. That's what you wanted to know isn't it? The land Captain Meredith bought is there, not in Jamaica. He's been working for it for years. Milking the profits by selling most slaves there, with only a token in Jamaica. He did it carefully at first, only a handful at a time, saving every shilling made. This last trip was a final reckoning. Maybe he got greedy – I don't know. Anyway he decided to complete his transactions once and for all – forty only sailing on to Spanish Town to make a token showing for the records. Now will you have done?'

All eyes turned to see him twisting his triangular hat as if that action alone was holding him together; his face white and despairing.

Joe Spriggs said: 'And you let yourself be a party to this? You're as guilty as he is.'

'How could I do otherwise? I'm in bondage to him to

the tune of three hundred guineas which he's squeezing me for, crushing me to death like a snake its prey.'

'But Mr Lascar – didn't he suspect?'

'Mr Lascar is dead. Buried at sea. The . . . flux is no respecter of persons.'

Joe Spriggs frowned, dissatisfied, and was preparing to ask a good many more questions when Miss Jarman cut in:

'The girl and the blackamoor can go. We've no more use for them. Meredith's due any time.' Any opportunity for learning more was gone. They were told to wait in the hall for the time being, until it was decided what should be done with them.

'The Cap'n's coming here – NOW!' Jess said urgently as the door closed and they were temporarily alone. 'It'll be the press gang for thee if we don't run off, and God knows what's for me without thee.'

He looked at her sharply and she realised what she'd said, but met his gaze determined not to go back on the promise to herself.

'Run off?' he said. 'What is in your mind?'

'Saving our skins,' she said holding fast to the plans that begged to be told, because there still wasn't enough time. 'Th'heard what she said – they've finished with us,' jerking her thumb at the closed door. 'Or near enough. Th'don't think that old harridan'll feed and clothe us till Kingdom Come? We've to look to ourselves . . . make a life for ourselves. Come on . . . now . . . before they finishes their arguing and it's too late!'

'Where do we go?' He was still suspicious and reluctant.

'To Mr Lambert's lodgings. There ain't nowhere else.' She was terrified that he would refuse, knowing she hadn't the strength to force him, and wouldn't even if she could. But he followed her as she went out into the street and the brown heat of the day, which steamed off the hot stone setts and fresh horse dung. Hawkins was dozing on his seat, the reins loose in his hands. He didn't see them hurry down the street and take the first turning that came: Jess talking and talking now. The ideas pushing and tumbling out in a fever of words that were scarcely intelligible.

'We'll scratch a living somehow. I ain't afraid of work. Maybe we could join the fair folk . . . prizefighting for thee and I'd be a tumbler. Th'didn't know I could do tricks did thee? Cartwheels, somersaults. I could learn others . . . if that Mr Randall ain't interested after all. But he must be. I heard all he said to the . . . though we could take a boat to France . . . they go regular. Or Lunnon. I've allus wanted to see it. Don't matter where . . . but it'ud be best if th'took to prizefighting. There's good money in that. Th'would be famous . . . think of it . . .' on and on and on, blithely unaware of the curious glances from the passers-by, though Midnight noticed every one. But neither of them saw Captain Meredith coming from the opposite direction on his way to visit Lawyer Loveitt, and he failed to see them as he crossed into Frog Lane seconds after they had left it.

Twelve

Church bells rang out over the sunlit streets of Bristol and across the two rivers where a fine evening haze spread, blurring the edges of the buildings, disguising flaws in paint and plaster, softening the impact of rags, heightening the charm of sprigged muslin and chintz. The man on the horse saw and wondered, just as he had when he came to a bend in the road outside the city and saw the panorama of classical buildings and the shining Avon. He gave a sudden shiver and his horse, sensitive to the rider's mood, stepped crablike towards the paving where a couple of chimney-boys were squatting on a doorstep. The man spoke quietly to the horse, soothing it. Both were tired. Their journey from London had taken several days and he was stiff and saddle sore, but he wanted to see more of this great city before finding an inn for the night. He took the horse down the steep winding streets to the waterfront.

Rich raw smells of tar, rotting excrement, spices and brine rose up along with the sight of ship masts, looped sails, small boats beached on the first mud of the receding tide, sailors in striped breeches and greasy caps leaning on the wooden railings, others arm in arm on their way to the taverns, piled kegs and crates, winches, the last of the horse-drawn sleds and – a gathering knot of people beyond a bonded warehouse. In the middle, a tall negro. Curiosity aroused, the rider turned his horse and rose towards them.

Jess saw him coming, but was too bothered by the

scrape she and Midnight were in to take any notice. Christmas! What had made her drag him down here? It was all her fault. She'd been lured by the old-fascination of ships and water, bored by the long fruitless wait outside James Lambert's lodgings, made nervous by the stares and comments and pointing fingers of passers-by. And now they were in a worse mess. He'd done no more than accidentally bump against some sailors aimlessly wandering from the passage next to the warehouse. He'd apologised but the sailors were already half cut.

'Clumsy black bastard. Didn't God give you eyes to use?'

'Did it a purpose . . . saw him, Paddy . . .'

'Jesus, Mary and Joseph – look at him! Walking with that lovely girleen. Hey darlin', don't you fancy me more than that nigger? I'll make your evening sparkle. Money in me pocket. See . . .' He'd pulled out a handful of coins, at the same time grabbing her shoulder, but Midnight had moved aside pulling Jess with him, and the other two men had hung on to the furious Paddy.

'I'll kill him, so I will. Just let me get at him!'

A few people stopped to watch. They were joined by others and a small crowd began to form, eager at the prospect of a fight. Jess had a sudden memory of the inn yard, of seeing Garty and Midnight. A crowd had come then to stare and cheer and lay bets – with the man Randall. But there wasn't a Randall now, only a lot of mildly hostile folk who were blocking the way, making running impossible.

'Let un go. Give the bugger a trouncing.'

'What's he done?'

'Punched the sailor without so much as a by th'leave! And all over that saucy trollop.'

'She's a tidy bit of stuff. I wouldn't mind taking up with

her . . .'

'Th'd better watch th'words, Jack, or th'missus'll give *thee* a trouncing!'

This brought a lot of laughter and people on the rim of the crowd pushed forward for a better look, squeezing the inside circle until there was no more room left for fighting, though Paddy had managed to free himself.

At this point Jess saw the horse and rider coming towards them, but her attention was on a voice behind her.

'Here . . . I know him. That's Cap'n Meredith's nigger. Aye, th'bist in right trouble now, Midnight. Cap'n's seething. Don't blame 'ee for running off, but th'best not get caught.' A man elbowed to the front of the crowd. He was short and broad with a veined red face and reddish corkscrew curls sprouting from under a woollen cap. Jess smelled gin as he grinned at her. They were all crushed against one another – Paddy at her side now. He was still cursing Midnight with great beery breaths, but had succeeded in finding her waist and was inching his hand up towards her breast. With great effort she managed to bend her arm and jab the point of her elbow in the soft pit of his stomach. What might've happened if the rider and horse hadn't arrived, mercifully she never discovered.

The horse was being encouraged forward. 'What is it? What has the African done?' The voice was quiet but authoritative with well-formed words.

'What's it to thee?' someone shouted, but already a few people had backed away from the horse, moving to a safer distance.

'It was a civil question,' the man said.

'He ain't done nothing and that's the truth,' Jess said, taking her first good look. She saw a quiet serious face, large dark eyes, well-marked brows, sober clothes. An air of authority.

'I see.'

Paddy knotted his fists again. 'He as good as tried to knock us down. Me and me shipmates. 'Tis never right him acting as if he owns the girleen. It's him as is owned. Cap'n Meredith's nigger slave, they say. And she as pretty as a picture with roses in her cheeks and the green eyes of a fairy.' He was fast becoming maudlin, sniffing now and rubbing the back of his hand under his nose.

'No man is owned by another,' the man said sternly.'

'Aw, come away, Paddy. We're losing good drinking time.' The two sailors took Paddy by his elbows, pulling him back towards the warehouse. He went reluctantly, scowling and cursing the man on the horse.

The man ignored him, his attention on Midnight. 'You live in Bristol?'

'At present. A traveller like yourself.'

A slight lift of the dark eyebrows was the only sign of surprise at the precise speech. 'A victim of the abominable slave trade?'

Midnight didn't reply, but Jess couldn't stop herself from saying: 'He were, but he ain't no longer. Why do thee ask?'

'I'm looking for anyone willing to talk about slaving. True histories of ship life. The treatment of slaves . . . anything and everything that happens from the time of enslavement in Africa through the the Middle Passage and the final sales and treatment in bondage.' He looked at Midnight. 'Perhaps you can give me experiences from your own life?'

Jess knew Midnight would shut like a clam at this direct request. She wanted to tell of the flogging he'd had, not in far off Jamaica, but here in England, but the forbidding frown and her own instinctive suspicion of strangers kept her silent.

The man looked from one to the other – waiting. 'If you've nothing to tell me,' he said at last, 'perhaps you will be good enough to direct me to the Friends' Meeting House?'

'Follow the river to Needless Gate. Cross it and the street will take you there.'

Jess gaped at the clear instruction. Midnight was forever filling her with surprises. She waited as he pointed up the quay, bursting to ask how he knew about the Quakers, let alone where they met.

The rider nodded, pulled the horse's head round. 'My thanks to you. Perhaps we may meet again. I shall be here for some time. Should you change your mind, the name is Clarkson. Thomas Clarkson. You can find me through the Friends,' and he pressed his horse's flanks, moving away at a steady pace.

'I never knew th'd even heard of the Quakers,' Jess said. 'How did th'know where they meet?'

'I take note of what surrounds me wherever I go.' Midnight was looking thoughtfully after the receding figure.

'He bist a queer un. Why do he want to know them things I wonder?'

The man with the corkscrew curls had been hanging round, listening and staring at Thomas Clarkson. He moved closer now, saying:

'Th'want to keep clear of such as he. That's the sort as'll turn thee over to the Cap'n as soon as look at thee . . . never mind his soft words.' He was looking Jess up and down. 'Hey, Midnight, tell us what th've been at. Isaac said th'must've drowned or got took by the press gang.'

'I've been minding my own business,' Midnight said curtly, putting his hand on Jess's shoulder.

145

'Right good business an'all. Not one of th'waterfront doxies.'

'Speak with care, Red.' He was even more curt and the man took a step back.

'I came to pass the time of day, that's all.' Red seemed anxious to put things straight. 'At Mike Mahoney's down in Marsh Street they were laying odds on thee having been cut up for cat's meat.' He laughed with a little more confidence. 'Know what I told 'em? Prizefighting, I says. That's what. Remember that time in Spanish Town? By . . . that was a fight to remember. I'll never forget how th'near slaughtered that feller – or the five gold guineas th'won for me off that dozy dago as set the Creole on thee. I've been a friend to thee ever since, haven't I, Midnight?' He nodded towards Jess. 'Make un tellee, miss. Allus stood by un I did. Not like Dando and them others. Prizefighting, I told 'em. They likes a good fight in Bristol. Plenty of chances for a lad as likely as thee. And there's money in it. Did thee see the miner from Kingswood last Saturday up on the Downs? Butcher Jem they called un. Brutal it were the way he knocked the other feller about.' He gave Midnight a nudge, not waiting for any answers. 'Whatever th'do, keep out of the Cap'n's sight till he gets his passage. The smoke fair streams from his ears when anyone mentions thee. If he was to catch thee, all thy fighting skills wouldn't be worth an ounce o' flea shit.'

'He won't,' Midnight said, keeping his eyes on Red and smiling coolly. 'Not if you hold your tongue.'

'Th'know me, Midnight. Old Red. Never let thee down. Never would.' He was backing away as he whined his protest. Hand half-raised he added: 'Don't forget it was me as told thee about Cap'n sailing for the Indies.'

Jess watched him turn and scurry away. She was left uneasy by something she didn't understand. An undercurrent of shared knowledge that was outside her experience. It was a shock realising she knew almost nothing of Midnight; all the worse because she'd let herself begin to depend on him. His hand was still firm on her shoulder and the contact changed from pleasure to a feeling she was nothing more than a possession. She didn't want that and wriggled free. But she didn't want that either and tried to smooth over any awkwardness by saying:

'That Red were afrighted. What did th'do?

Midnight shrugged, not wanting to talk about the old slave days in Spanish Town or Montserrat, walking her along, keeping clear of the last idling stragglers. The incident was over. Finished. Leaving their position depressingly obvious. He blamed himself for letting Jess persuade him into running off. They should have stayed. Observed the words and faces of the English pigs. Then acted. He'd broken his rule. Put his plan in danger. And all because of this English girl who wasn't a pig. He looked at her, aware she was equally ill at ease; aware also how much he'd grown to depend on her. She'd soothed the terrible empty fear and loneliness. Now it came back twice as strong at the thought of losing her. He recognised the feeling was in danger of becoming a passion, but a passion already in decay – mildewed by the awful distrust he could not root out. Why had he picked a white girl? But there hadn't been a choice. It had quietly happened. A marvel and a disaster. He should be grappling with the problem of how to stay alive, but instead could think of nothing but the problem of Jess. To take his mind away from it, he said:

'Well, and have you decided? You are the master.'

'I ain't nobody's master,' she said with the slight thrust of her jaw which always amused and moved him.

'Mistress then.'

'I ain't nobody's mistress neither.' She blushed because of his quizzical look which said a great deal and turned everything topsy turvy and her knees to water, leaving her in a worse confusion. 'We'd best try the lodgings again. We'll knock this time.' She didn't feel that brave, but anything was better than hanging about to no purpose. 'Mr Lambert has to go home sometime.'

'And if he doesn't?'

'Then we'll have to find that Randall on our own. Do th'think as Red 'ud know him?'

'Why should he? I have not your confidence, Jess. Are you always not so sure in yourself?'

'Course not! But it ain't no good moping. Besides, if th'bustles enough, folk give way and things get done.' And it was all so much eyewash to keep up their spirits. James Lambert wouldn't be there.

But he was, and looked astounded when the housekeeper of the lodgings – a suspicious woman in greening black clothes, a dirty mob cap on her sparse hair – called him to the door of the gabled house.

'Madness!' he said, when Jess explained what they were after. 'Quite impossible . . . but don't stand in the street.' He was looking about apprehensively; looking anywhere but directly at them.

They stepped into the dingy passage. The housekeeper hovered in the background looking very distrustful and Jess began to wish they'd never come.

'Mr Randall said . . .' she began again, but James Lambert interrupted her.

'Oh, Randall . . . you don't want to take much notice of him. He fancies himself as a sporting man.' He gave a little laugh. 'Besides, I haven't seen him in weeks. He's no good to you. A man of ever-changing whims, and now I see you're freed from your fearful collar, Midnight, you'd do better to sign on. There's plenty of call for deckhands in the navy. Keep you out of Miss Jarman's clutches and the Captain's. You caused a minor earthquake vanishing like that.' He turned on the housekeeper with ill-concealed irritation: 'There's no need to wait, Mrs Gossage. I'll see these people out.'

She went reluctantly, and he added in a low voice: 'I can't help you I'm afraid. I've the problems of the world on my shoulders and the Captain snapping at my heels. There's no money to stake you - it's gone towards paying my debts . . . a drop in the ocean.'

The threatening cloud of gloom that had been peasized when they'd set out for Host Street grew to storm proportions. Jess felt swamped. How Midnight felt, she didn't know. He was standing quietly and hadn't spoken at all. She was surprised when he said:

'Is there no means by which I can find Mr Randall? I am determined to consult with him.'

James Lambert sighed heavily. 'I suppose you could try the Hatchett Inn if you won't take my advice. When his mind's on fisticuffs he sits in on the training sessions there. But if you do find him, for God's sake only mention my name when no one else is within earshot. There's nothing more I can do for you.' He was moving forward, opening the door. As they passed him, he looked directly at Midnight for the first time and said with genuine feeling: 'I'm sorry. No ill feeling?'

'None,' Midnight replied, and went out with Jess into the street.

They walked side by side, not touching, down to the corner where Steep Street began. It's going to be all right – Jess told herself as they turned and began to climb. Keep on being bold, like with the old baggages.

Thirteen

'Bundle do th'say?' repeated the serving wench over the tap-room noise.

'Randall. Mr Randall.' Jess looked anxiously at the round red face that seemed made for smiles, but was frowning now.

The girl pushed past, her hands full of brimming tankards. 'Here let us set these down first – afore I drops 'em.'

They were in the smoky tap-room of the Hatchett Inn, where light pushed with difficulty through the haze, revealing wooden settles and tables ringed with beer stains. Heads were turning. Curious stares and nudges. Jess felt herself sweating. The heat travelling in waves along her arms, up her neck, and into her face. It was their last chance. If it failed . . .

'Mr Randall th'say?' The girl had come back. 'He were here not long since, but I don't know whether he stayed. Does he know thee?' She was staring nervously at Midnight as if he were a strange animal. She seemed to think him deaf as well, because she elbowed Jess asking: 'Do Mr Randall know him an' all?' with such amazement that Jess felt like hitting her.

'That's why we've come. On business!' the last very firmly with Lawyer Loveitt importance.

'I dunno . . .'The girl was doubtful, her instincts all against this unlikely pair.

151

'It ain't for thee to know. Is he or ain't he? And if he ain't I'll speak to the landlord.' Lord knows where she'd found the nerve to talk so, but the girl seemed impressed.

'Th'd better try the back room, where Jem's training. Out that door and along the passage. The noise'll tell thee where to go.'

Midnight followed Jess obediently. He'd hardly spoken a word since they'd walked away from Host Street, and Jess had been too wrapped in her own strange state of mind to notice the dividing wall of silence. She noticed now. He seemed in a dream and when she said:

'Th'do think it's the right thing to do, don't thee?' he didn't answer.

It was dark in the passage though the day was not over. They could hear the ebb and flow of voices and an occasional grunt of effort. At the door, Jess hung back, the last of her bravery eaten up in getting this far, and it was Midnight who lifted the latch. The door opened into a low-ceilinged room that was almost empty of furniture, but seemed filled with men. Two were sitting on a bench with their backs to a diamond-paned window, shadows against the last of the daylight. Others leaned against the wall, attention concentrated on the pugilists in the centre of the room. They were stripped to the waist and barefoot; circling each other; fists raised chest high; while a third man – a powerful stocky individual whose several chins overflowed his shirt neck – urged them on with his advice.

Lit as he was by direct window light, the effect of Midnight's entrance was dramatic. The man with the chins said:

'Who said thee could come in here?' with such aggression that he momentarily distracted one of the fighters, who lowered his guard for a fraction of time. It was enough. A quick jab left and right, and he was flat on his back with such an expression of dazed surprise, that Jess, coming in behind Midnight, wanted to laugh.

'Give over, Jem. That weren't sporting.'

The ox of a man spat on the floor and shrugged. 'Tommy's a bloody fool,' he said. 'Never could keep his mind on what he's doing. I've told thee afore, Mat, it's like sparring with a piece o' wet rag!'

The man getting up from the floor began protesting, but Mat cut him short: 'Shut up! And thee!' as Jem opened his mouth. 'I asked thee a question,' he was glaring at Midnight.

'I am looking for Mr Randall, but I see he is not present.'

'Left half an hour back, so th'can bugger off and take the wench with thee.'

'You wish for someone new to spar with?' Midnight spoke directly to Jem. 'I will fight you.'

'Thee!' There was a snort of laughter from one of the men sitting on the window bench. Someone else said, 'He's game anyway. Give him a chance.'

'It's what I came for,' Midnight said. 'On Mr Randall's advice I want to try the sport.'

'Hark at him! "Try the sport" . . . black as me hat and talking like a fop. Get back in the bilge or the bawdy house . . . that's where th'belongs.'

'Afeared, Jem?' said the same supporter who had asked for a chance – a little bald man, propped against the wall.

Jem spun round, his broad stubbly face the colour of boiled lobster, his pig eyes screwed up threateningly. 'Th'd better mind th'words or I'll show you what I can do. Here, get th'coat off, nigger! Th'wants a fight, do thee . . .' He loomed forward, head hunched between a mountain of shoulder muscle, punching with his great lumpy fist. Midnight coughed, unable to help retreating. 'Want to spar . . . do thee . . . try the . . . sport . . .' Jem spat out the words between jabs.

'Jem Tudge – GIVE OVER!' bawled Mat, shoving hard enough to shift Jem off course. 'And thee . . . get th'black hide out of here!

Midnight didn't waste time with words. Slipping out of his coat he thrust it at Jess, then peeled off his shirt. He'll be slaughtered – she thought aghast, admiring and wanting to interfere all at the same time. The other was as tall and broader. She looked at Midnight's dusky back, saw the muscle separation making dark moving valleys and lighter hills; shoulders and biceps knotting and rippling. There was a tension . . . a determination about him that held her back.

Jem had thrown off Mat's restraining bulk and came at Midnight, who slid away, drawing him back into the middle of the room. There were shouts of:

'Move Tommy . . . give un space . . . go on, hit un, Blackie . . . that's it, Jem, none of th'rabbit punches. A good solid thump . . .'

For Jess it was a nightmare of her own creating. She didn't want to watch, but couldn't keep her eyes off the fighters. It wouldn't have been so bad if they'd been sparring in a friendly way, but there was spleen in this. She'd seen plenty of brawls and blood, but this was so unfair. Butcher Jem was twice as heavy as Midnight, and his pride had been hurt. She looked at the curling mat of hair that covered shoulders and chest. It was a distinct contrast to the smooth black body that shone with a first fine sweat. Speed and clever footwork was all that kept off disaster and let in a few first successful punches. She heard Midnight grunt with effort and the smack of knuckles on flesh, but it seemed no more forceful than a gnat flying head on into a carthorse. And he hadn't staying power.

Couldn't have after those weeks of illness. Waves of the tiredness he must be experiencing seemed to wash over her. She felt the first of Jem's punches connect as if with her own ribs. A second punch and Midnight stumbled. Oh Lordy, we need some ghosty stuff to scare un off, or a fireball to fly in through the window. She was hugging his coat and shirt tight against her, the scent of him coming poignant into her nostrils. Lie down . . . for pity's sake lie down, or th'will be murdered! But what was she doing acting like a traitor? She should be cheering him on. No one else would.

'Keep it up, me love. He ain't as quick as thee. It's the nippy ones as'll do more damage. Quick . . . that's it. Go on . . . another jab . . .'

A snigger of laughter greeted Jess's shouts. The little man who had first encouraged Midnight called out:

'The wench is as sporty as her man. What do th'say, Mat? Randall knows quality when he sees it. If it's true he told the blackamoor to try his hand, then he's a likely winner.'

'Dunno . . . too early to tell,' Mat said, chins quivering as he watched Midnight land another punch that did no more than raise a grunt.

Tell 'em to stop, Jess was begging inside, though she knew it was a betrayal. Her entreaty seemed to have an effect.

'That's enough, lads,' Mat said. 'JEM! Got cloth ears have thee?' Another sickening blow and Midnight staggered back. Mat put himself between them. 'Cool down, will thee! It ain't no fight to the death.'
Midnight was breathing heavily, the muscles of his chest and stomach heaving.

'Th'bist out of condition,' Mat said. 'And too thin. But game enough and keen. I'll give thee a chance.

Daresay Mr Randall will like to see what th'can do. Can th'come every night for training?'

'Yes. All day as well.'

Mat looked at him with a frown of suspicion. 'Who are thee? What's th'name?'

'They call me Midnight. Nothing else matters.'

But Mat was looking at him with sudden interest. 'Do th'know of Cap'n Meredith?' he asked.

Midnight looked at him coolly. 'I know the name and something of the man.'

'They were talking down at the Seven Stars about a runaway slave.'

One of the other men butted in eagerly: 'That's it, Mat . . . Landlord Thompson was on about him . . . th'know as how he won't have aught to do with the slavers. This un *must* be him.'

They were all staring now; conversations left hanging in the air.

'There ain't slaves in England,' Jess said abruptly, giving Midnight his shirt. 'And he's here, ain't he? So how can he be runaway or a slave?'

'I was once a slave,' Midnight said.

'It'ud draw the crowds, Mat,' said the little man. 'Think of it "Battling Black versus Butcher Jem" . . . they'd come from miles off, specially if they knew he were a slave.'

'I don't fancy trouble. I've heard tales of that Cap'n Meredith.'

'What can he do with Jem to protect thee?'

'Laughter gusted out, curling round the walls. Jem said:

'I ain't his bodyguard and I'll make damn sure I keep from coming here if Mat tries setting me up against this black monkey. Who does he think he is with his fancy talk and his waterfront whore . . .'

He didn't get any further. Midnight turned, right fist

knotted, arm coming down in that same short deadly punch that had flattened Garty. And Jem was slumped at his feet. So swift; so unexpected was the action that even Mat was taken aback. With a great snort of laughter he slapped Midnight's back.

'I'd never have believed it if I hadn't seen it with me own eyes . . . never in all me born days. Taken his senses proper!' He kneeled by Jem. 'Wet the towel someone and give it to me.' As he squeezed water over the unconscious Jem, he said to Midnight: Th'can stay for now if th'has a mind. I'll find summat for thee to do. Food and somewhere to sleep, that's all. Show what th'bist made of and money'll come. There's a fat enough purse for any pug as can give a good account of himself. For tonight there's hay in the stable. Th'can doss down there.'

Midnight looked at Jess. 'Both of us?'

Mat straightened up, still on his knees. 'Hold on now, I ain't supporting the poor of the parish! If she's nowhere to go there's always the Old Mint.'

'I ain't going there. Not if I were dying,' Jess said.

'Aw, let her sleep with the hosses tonight anyway, Mat. Where's the harm?' The little man gave her a meaning wink.

'I don't know about that. There's this little problem to settle. Better use th'strength on this bloody great carcass, Midnight. Throw some water over the bugger; we've to bring back his wits somehow. That's it. Now . . . heave . . .'

Not accepted, but not dismissed, Jess watched them struggle to get Butcher Jem sitting on a bench. It seemed no time since they'd stepped into this room and a new life. She should be over the moon. It was the chance she'd wanted for him – for them both. Instead she felt chilled.

*

It was warm in the stable. And dark. Jess was glad of that. Lines of moonlight drew the shape of the door. A broader sheet of silver spread from a small window high in the wall. All but one of the stalls were occupied. They had put a good thick layer of straw down in the empty stall and were sitting there, leaning against the wooden partition. The horses whickered softly and blew, with the occasional stamp and scrape of a hoof. A sweet earthy smell surrounded them. Away from the noise of the inn; alone with Midnight for the first time since that extraordinary morning, Jess felt suddenly shy. As if she was to bed with a stranger. But it wasn't like that. Had Midnight been a stranger she would never have stayed. Better to sleep in some corner of an alley like before, than to give herself to someone she didn't know. Though that didn't seem to be the way of things – sitting so quiet as they were. She took a sly peek at Midnight, seeing his dark shape, made darker by the shadows. He was after all a stranger. The thought brought a shiver with it.

'Cold, Jess?'

'Can you see me that well?' she asked, surprised.

'Well enough.'

Talking had broken through some of her shyness. She was able to say: 'I'm that pleased for thee. But scared as well.'

'Why scared?'

'Because th'will get mangled. 'Twas no more than a piece of luck flattening that great ox. If he'd seen thee coming it 'ud've been thee licking the dust off the floor.'

'A strange encouragement!' but he was laughing and the warmth of the sound eased the constraint. He took her hand. 'It would never have happened if you had not been there. So you can see the real piece of luck is having found such a friend.'

Now the shyness came sweeping back. It was as if layers of everyday cover were being peeled back from them both. She felt excited and a little afraid. The whole day had been astonishing. Enough packed in it to last a year. Part of her wanted to run, but she did nothing, leaving her hand where it was.

He said softly: 'You don't know what it means to find work outside slavery. Bloody work though it is. Not to be ordered about like a cur. Any beatings now will be of my own seeking . . . my own choice. I've been whipped many times for trivial reasons, oversleeping and arriving late in the field, for arrogance, for no more reason than Gomer's whim . . . and he whipped for pleasure.' He paused, interrupted by memory. Jess wanted to ask what he was thinking, but the tense attitude of his body stopped her. 'Work and breeding,' he said in a low voice. 'That is all the slave animal is fitted for. Slave!' The word came out with so much bitter disgust that he shivered. He put a hand to his bare neck. No more collar. Free. At liberty. But what use are words? How can I describe the feeling . . . how can I make you understand? It spreads there . . . and there . . .' He pressed his hand over his heart and then on his forehead.

Moved, she said: 'I do understand,' wanting to explain that her own life had not been so very different, but unable to find the right words. Honesty forced her to add: 'But there's other things as important,' thinking that earning bread to keep from starving was the thing that counted in the end.

'Nothing . . . not food nor warmth nor family . . . *nothing* is as important as throwing off slavery.' He spoke so passionately she was silenced, though still not quite convinced. 'Dignity is returned to me. The world must take me as an equal man.'

Now she couldn't keep quiet: 'Th'bist truly daft, if th'thinks that! D'thee imagine the old toffee-nosed Jarman and that stuffed lot as own the *Princess* 'ud ever accept thee or me as their equals?' If only Mat and Jem and the rest of them could look in now – she thought – see us sitting so prim . . . *talking*! Laughter bubbled in her throat.

Midnight said: 'You know that I'm no simpleton. It doesn't matter what other people have in their minds. To me it's like unloading the weight of the world from my shoulders.' He let go her hand and sprang up. 'See, I'm six feet taller! Tall enough to reach the sky and pick the stars and the moon, even though you think I'm a fool. Being free! Oh Jess . . . being free . . .' and he grasped both her hands this time, pulling her up, whirling her around in a crazy dance till she was dizzy, with no breath left to tell him she'd been laughing at something quite different.

The straw laced around their feet, kicking up in small tufts, hindering them until they collapsed. Even then Midnight wasn't satisfied. 'To be indoors is wrong. We should be under the sky with a fire burning and a feast and real dancing. A celebration that would please the god of the sun and his moon wife. Drums to make your feet leap and leap.' He began to clap – a slow quiet insistent pulse that passed to his feet allowing his hands freedom to play stronger, more complicated beats which enchanted her. She wanted to join in, but was afraid of not being able to keep the exact time.

Without being told, he understood and said: 'It needs two. Clap with me . . .'

They went back to the beginning, Jess stumbling a little, the tension of not wanting to fail bringing failure. Gradually she became more confident and relaxed, keeping a slow accurate beat going so that we was able to begin the decorations again, developing into an intricate pattern of sound that filled her ears, head, body; flowing through her limbs; prickling the hairs on the nape of her neck. The whole world was in this marvellous rhythm.

At last he stopped. 'We'll rouse the house. The horses are restless already.'

She hadn't noticed and lay back in the straw, listening to the snorting and the flicking of head and mane. Midnight settled quietly beside her. He neither spoke nor offered to touch her and she felt strangely disconcerted. She could hear him breathing fast and deep; feel the straw moving between them as if it was carrying a force that ran into her body making her skin buzz. The sense of release brought about by the clapping died and she became aware of the bones of her bodice digging uncomfortably into her waist and constricting her ribs. Was he going to lie there for ever and just go to sleep? Who was going to make the first move? She sighed, sat up and began to ease the lacing, meaning to slip smoothly and efficiently out of bodice, skirt, petticoat and blouse, leaving only her shift. But the lace knotted and she couldn't see well enough to unpick it. Her hands were sweaty, and feeling thoroughly hot and awkward, she tugged. The lace refused to budge and in desperation she tried to pull the bodice as it was over her head. It reached the point where her arms stuck straight up, and then she was truly wedged.

'Oh Lordy . . . I'd never do much as a whore!' she said, muffled and despairing. 'Get me out!'

There was a shout of laughter and she felt the bodice eased away. Midnight said: 'Who asked for a whore? It's you I want.'

She emerged flustered and red-faced, scraping at her hair which had become loose and insisted in standing out round her head like wild unsheared sheep-wool. 'Me?' she said weakly, as if she hadn't known all along and been aching for him in return.

'You!' and putting his arms around her he pulled her into the comfort of the hay.

Fire ran through her veins. For a time she forgot everything but the life of her body. Extraordinary half-known sensations flowered under his touch, driving her to throw away all the old fears in a marvellous spontaneous joy, that at first she was sure must be theirs alone, and then wondered if it was shared by the couples she'd seen locked together in dark waterfront alleys? The wonder of it grew. Her mind divided. One half drowning in delicious physical glory, the other separate and thinking – so this is how it feels – as her hair, skin, breasts were caressed. Ecstatic and slightly scared, she revelled in the smooth steel of his body, the pressure of thigh on thigh, the honey-mouth taste, the smell of cloves and salt, which rose to a climax and melted all apprehension. Even the discomfort as he drove into her was a small price to pay for the abandoned animal joy.

Afterwards Midnight looked at Jess lying so quietly in his arms, and was astonished by what he'd done. Taboo had been swept aside, but among the confusion of triumph, doubt, joy, distrust, there was not one drop of guilt. She'd broken through all his defenses, given him concern, laughter, her body; allowed him to be a man. All this willingly. He wondered if he loved her in the way of a white man, and put his hand on her hair, pushing his fingers through the coarse strands.

She opened her eyes, smiling. 'That were good. I never knew it would be.'

An ocean of tenderness threatened his calm. He knew he was totally vulnerable. She'd made him so, and a tiny thorn of resentment pricked him.

'I do love thee,' she said cheerfully, not knowing anything of this resentment and adding to it by producing even greater tenderness.

To combat the unwelcome conflict and because he wanted desperately to strengthen the bond between them, Midnight thought of sharing even more of himself, to close the gap that still separated them. An intolerable gap of birth and upbringing. Should he put himself to even greater risk? He decided to take the chance and began telling her about his old tribal life and the easy-going happiness destroyed so hideously by the slavers. How they tramped mile upon mile in the slave coffle, down to Calabar and the dungeons by the sea. Days spent waiting to board the terrible slave ships. The horror of the Middle Passage, where he'd been tempted to kill himself and had resisted, only to face worse horrors in the sugar plantations.

'But th'said th'were a house slave,' Jess remarked, concealing the agony of listening to these things when her whole being was alert and tender.

'That was later. When I was sold to Mr Sanderson.'

'Who branded thee.' She resented any suggestion of affection for this master.

'Who taught me English and opened the world of books. He was almost blind, you understand. Someone had to read to him. Jacob, the old slave who'd been his eyes before, was ailing, and he said I was quick to learn so he passed on his knowledge, teaching me to read and write . . . be my Master's right hand.'

'And what did thee read?'

'Novels, poetry, plays, letters. He was much favoured of Shakespeare, Homer's Iliad, the *Song of Solomon*, the new poet William Blake . . . "Tyger Tyger burning bright in the forests of the night. What immortal" . . .'

Jess put a hand over his mouth, suddenly jealous of this wealth of knowledge denied her. 'All those names,' she said. 'Me brain's in knots!'

He pulled her hand away and kissed her.

She rolled from him, still disturbed, wanting to talk about something she understood. 'When they wed in thy village, what do they do?'

'No more and no less than what we've done.'

'No . . . no. I mean afore! There ain't no churches nor no parsons to seal the troth.'

'No, but we have a great feast, after the bride has arrived with her dowry of cattle and household goods and all her relatives. Blessings and dances are performed. Everyone is happy. We drink palm wine and sing.'

'Do th'put a wedding ring on her finger?'

'Our marriage mark is a girdle of string.'

'We might manage that, if th'was willing,' Jess said, burying her face in his shoulder.

'What?'

'A piece of string. There's some in me pocket. I saved it from last Sunday's goose. We ain't got money for gold rings.'

He shook with laughter again, hold her tight so the feel of the laughter ran into her body. When he could get breath he said: 'You wait. I'll load your fingers with rings. We'll travel . . . see many lands. Go home to the Eboe; to my country.'

'Us, together,' she said, glad to take part in this dandelion dream. She had been so afraid she had gone too far.

'Together,' he agreed. 'I'll fight the whole world if I have to.'

'Midnight . . .' she began, but this time it was his hand

that covered her mouth.

'Olaudah – I said I might share my name with you one day, do you remember?'

'*Olaudah.*' She tried it out, liking the full sound.

'It means of good fortune,' he said wryly. 'I never believed it until now.'

She felt the tears come and was choked. The great happiness was suddenly, inexplicably threatened and a voyage to Africa became a threat. Closing her eyes she lay still, curled up against him, feigning sleep until it came.

Fourteen

Randall stood in the coolest part of the Hatchet Inn yard watching Midnight punching a sack packed tight with straw. The sack was secured to a bracket on the wall of the inn and swung and twisted under the heavy blows.

'Broughton's rules,' he said to Mat who was standing beside him out of the July heat. 'It's time someone lifted prizefighting from the fairground mud, and how better than by applying the ruling of such a magnificent pugilist as Jack Broughton?'

'He ain't Jack Broughton or another Jim Figg for that matter – hadn't th'noticed?' Mat said sarcastically. 'He's only a nigger with a bit o'talent.'

'You miss the point.' Randall adjusted his stock, then smoothed the skirt of his well-cut coat. The day was hot, but he chose to remain fully and impeccably clothed, unlike Mat and the hangers-on in shirts with rolled sleeves and open necks, or Midnight stripped to the waist and oiled with sweat.

Jess came out from the inn kitchen carrying a jug of ale to quench Midnight's thirst when the training was over. She put it down by the wall on top of the covered water butt and stopped to admire. The hard beauty of him turned her heart over. What a piece of luck they'd come here! Or was it luck? She couldn't help a creeping sense of pride. It had been her persistence that had brought them this far – and Midnight's skill if she was honest.

Without it they'd never have been absorbed into the life of the inn as ostler and kitchen wench. It was a good life even if Mat's wife was a bit of a scold and the work took all their waking hours, making it hard to snatch any time. She sighed. Sometimes their half-life together was so frustrating she was tempted to urge him to join the fair folk, but held back knowing it would wreck their chances. Out of the corner of her eye she saw Randall take a fine white kerchief from his pocket and dab his nose like a lady. She suppressed a giggle and listened to him saying:

'I've made the final arrangements. A portion of the fairground in Horsefair is allotted to the fight, but it isn't going to be any booth brawl! A cut above that. I want it to be a match of consequence. I've had a soundly constructed canvas shed erected that will hold two hundred people if it rains, and many more if it doesn't and we can roll up the sides. A raised stage inside, well roped with plenty of room for the square of a yard to be chalked just as Broughton recommends. Care to take a stroll down when Midnight's done . . . that's if Mrs Mat will spare you from your duties?' He looked at Mat in a way that made the innkeeper growl:

'Course I'll come. I'm me own man, not a hen-pecked babby!'

Midnight stopped work, relaxing his arms, stretching and flexing the muscles of his back. 'I would also like to view the stage,' he said.

Randall questioned Mat with his eyebrows.

'Oh I daresay it'll be all right. I'll have a word with the wife,' Mat said, contradicting himself.

Jess sighed again. Another chance gone. He'd not be back before the evening rush of serving customers, preparing food, running errands, collecting empties, washing up and eventual exhausted sleep.

Midnight heard, understood and said softly: 'It will not be so for ever. Two days more and that fifteen guinea purse will be mine. The start of our fortune, Jess.' He was smiling and looking so happy, she had to smile back, even though something stopped her from wholeheartedly sharing his confidence. He really believes he'll win – she thought. All along he'd been certain of success, unlike his usual reserved doubtful attitude to most things. She felt ashamed of such lack of faith and said:

'Don't take any notice of me. I'm just crotchety because they're stealing our time.'

He caught her as she went towards the door of the inn and gave her a resounding kiss. She was astonished, because he'd never been so free in front of an audience. There was a ribald cheer and her face flamed, but she returned the kiss, defiantly putting her arms round his neck to make sure everyone would mark and remember.

'I know th'will win,' she said into his neck, and then pulled away to run and hide her blushes indoors.

'Th'can whip some raw eggs for th'sweetheart's supper,' If he's to win we must keep his wind sound.'

*

Horsefair was thronging with people – all of Bristol and more on the streets in holiday mood. Taverns and their fair-time makeshift counterparts, the bush houses, were doing a roaring trade. Satisfied customers reeled into the fresh air and slid into snoring sleep on the stone steps. Midnight pushed through, Jess and Mat close behind. Already the Pie Poudre court that was held in front of the Merchant's Tolzey had dispensed some instant justice. They'd seen one man in the stocks and three others handbolted, being carried off to Newgate by the bailiffs.

Jess wondered what they'd done. Brawling most like, or dipping into pockets that weren't their own! She'd got behind and made a sudden spurt to catch up, feeling the sun beat down on her head and shoulders, envying Midnight who revelled in the burning weather.

Two weeks of no rain had dried out the streets and little skirls of dust rose round Midnight's feet. Hot sun struck through to his skin, patching his shirt with sweat, massaging his muscles. The day was his! He could feel it and was joyful. He'd slay the Butcher, which would please Jess, and for himself he would have proved to the world that the slave was as much a man as any of them. With that thought came another, sour and dispiriting – what did fighting ever prove? He was going to be a sideshow for the holiday makers to stare at; nothing more. He looked across the fairground where piled stalls were partially hidden by a dense crush of people. Only the wares strung high under canvas roofs were visible. Crisp bright prints billowed like loose sails in the small hot wind. Ribbons and laces fluttered. A row of gingerbread men were hung by the neck, their currant eyes blindly bulging.

Coming up behind, Jess slotted her arm through his, pointing to a rough platform in front of a curtained booth where a painted woman in short full skirts was bawling for custom:

'A play the like of which you of which you've never seen. Murder dark and deadly to make your blood curdle and raise the hairs on your heads. Even your wigs won't be safe, ladies and gents . . . walk up, walk up . . .'

'Don't th'wish th'could go in?' Jess said.

He squeezed her arm to his side. 'I've a better show to give.' He was fairly bouncing with confidence now. Even the sight of a mangy bear, collared and chained, didn't raise the earlier discouraging thought. And as if to set a seal on his confidence, he caught sight of the generous red flag fluttering on a pole beyond the acting booth.

'See . . . that's our tent,' he told Jess.

'I'll be glad when we reach it. I could do with summat to wet me whistle,' Mat puffed, catching them up. 'Seen aught of Jem yet?'

Midnight shook his head, and Jess said: 'He'll be the one wetting his whistle if I knows anything. He'd drink the sea dry if he could!'

'The more booze in him the better for our purpose!'

'I don't need help to conquer him,' Midnight protested.

Mat laughed and wiped a sweaty arm across his sweatier forehead. 'Keep th'boasting till after . . . by all that's holy, if Mr Randall ain't laid on some ale, I'll . . .' he didn't say what, and barged on into the crowd.

They were almost at the tent. People were beginning to take notice, nudging and pointing. There was a bill advertising the fight, tacked to one of the support posts. A crude portrait of Midnight and Butcher Jem – gawky black spider man and vast white gorilla on spindle legs; stiff arms raised; fists clenched – underneath in bold black capitals:

BUTCHER JEM THE KINGSWOOD MINER
WILL THIS DAY FIGHT IN UNLIMITED ROUNDS
MIDNIGHT THE BATTLING BLACK
FROM THE GUINEA COAST

Randall pushed through the tent flaps, as cool and dandified in appearance as ever. He seemed in good spirits and greeted Midnight with:

'What do you think to our portrait then? Excellent wouldn't you say? A touch thin, but then what can you expect from a hack printer!' and he laughed – a high rattling sound that irritated Jess. She said indignantly:

'It ain't like him at all. He ain't no more like a stick

than that big ape.'

'Let us hope all your supporters are as loyal,' Randall said.

Jess suspected he was making fun of her frowned, but didn't dare say anything rude because he was the gaffer. It was his money backing the fight.

Midnight said unconcerned: 'It is well enough and tells the crowd where to come.' He went into the tent and Jess followed, still amazed by his assurance. Didn't he have any nerves? Apparently not! She watched him go to the stage, climb up and walk round with a bouncy movement as if testing his own responses.

'He's cool enough,' Mat said admiringly. 'Th'd never know he was a novice.'

Jess remembered Red and his talk of the fight in Spanish Town, but didn't say anything. If they liked to think of him as new to the game, so much the better. She looked round. A few men were talking together on the far side of the tent, and behind the stage the canvas sides were already being rolled to let air into the stifling heat. Mat walked off and Midnight climbed down. He came back to her and as they both had their backs to the flaps, neither of them saw James Lambert come in. The first they knew of his presence was a hand on Midnight's shoulder, and an edgy voice saying:

'I was hoping for a quick word before the fight. Private, if you will forgive me.' He was looking at Jess and she could do nothing but move away, wondering at his evident brittle nervousness.

'I've a favour,' James said when she was out of earshot. 'Come over here.' He propelled Midnight to an airless corner. There was a cracking tension that communicated through his hand. 'Swift,' he muttered. 'Time's scarce as diamonds.'

'What is it?'

'I've the weight of the world in debt – you probably know. The bailiffs are hunting me down. Over a thousand I owe – five hundred in guineas to Captain Meredith . . .' In spite of his declared urgency he hesitated.

'Go on!' Midnight began to unbutton his shirt.
'Forgive my frankness, but we are old friends. This is your first fight – in England anyway. You are young . . . have plenty of time . . . there will be other fights; other chances . . .'

Midnight cut through the circles: 'Speak your mind.'

'I ask you to forfeit this fight.'

The rushed words seemed to slow down and hang like poised swords. Midnight became very still.

'It's my liberty I'm asking for. A favour for a favour . . . remember Billy Waring? Someone had to lose. You will win many other times . . . because we're friends . . .'

'Friends!' The word burst from Midnight. He felt physically sick and turned his back, ripping off his shirt, beginning his warming-up exercises in a fierce attempt to quieten his raging emotions. He must get back his calm – think only of the fight. Go over the strategy. Consider his attack. There was no room at all for blind anger.

'It's my last wager, I promise. I need only enough to buy me a passage for Montserrat.'

'Montserrat?' Midnight swung round. 'And when you arrive there, what then?'

James said awkwardly: 'I've a position promised as overseer.' Then with a rush: 'If it's the purse that worries you, I will give you fifteen guineas from my winnings.'

The pattern of events half-realised in Midnight's mind, along with a sense of insult more painful than a flogging. But there was no time left for talk. Butcher Jem had swaggered in with his seconds and Mat was hurrying over as the tent flaps were tied back, letting in the crowd.

Jess came round the corner of the stage where she had been lingering, hoping to eavesdrop. The only word she had heard clearly was 'Montserrat', but the look on Midnight's face was one she knew – cold and shut in. She felt angry and glared at James Lambert, wanting to ask what had been said that was so upsetting, but people were flocking round. She had time only to say: 'Good luck!' as Midnight ducked under the rope, pulling himself on to the stage.

From the back of the tent a voice shouted: 'The slave's up . . . ain't he a big bugger!'

Behind Jess another voice answered: 'He's naught but cats-meat. Jem'll eat un!'

'Then he'll be eating his usual fare . . .'

The banter went on while the men in the ring got ready; moving into the chalk square with the umpire; sizing each other – Midnight unblinking; the Butcher red-faced and sweating from the ale he'd already drunk.

The umpire said something quietly. His arm came down and he moved back. The Butcher struck out and the crowd cheered because the fight had begun, but Midnight stepped out of reach, then back to jab with his left fist once . . . twice, each time twisting away from trouble. The small nagging painful blows enraged Jem and set him lumbering forward, an awesome wicked sight; his tree-trunk arms swinging viciously.

Below, pushed close to the stage, Jess had a steeply angled view. She could see Midnight's white stockings turned over at the knees – an inch of ebony flesh and then his grey breeches, allowing for ease of movement. His legs and body moved with quick control, shifting out of sight behind the great sweating hairy bulk of Jem, then back again; their feet pounding on the drum of the stage. The scars on Midnight's back were clearly visible, oiled and silvery. Suddenly the shaved bull head when down between the massive shoulders and Jem charged. Jess saw Midnight turn aside, but not quick enough. The Butcher's shoulder slammed into his ribs with a fearful shudder. Midnight slipped and fell back winded, burning his scars on the rope, then hauling on it to right himself.

Involuntarily Jess cried out, but remembering she was here to cheer him on, yelled:

'Don't let un wrestle thee . . .' as Jem tried to hook an arm over the back of Midnight's neck, 'duck down . . . that's it . . . that's it . . .'

Behind her men were shouting: 'Do for un, Jem . . . break his black bones and we'll chop un for thee.'

But Jem didn't seem to hear, and Midnight curling his body under and up, brought down a lightning blow that caught Jem on the side of the jaw before he could straighten up. He rocked. The crowd roared, and from behind came a chorus of boos. Glancing round, Jess saw faces seamed and lined with black. Miners! Jem's pit mates, and she was standing in front! She started to edge away, but the crowd was packed so tight there was nowhere to go. More transfixing that that was a glimpse of a white face, unmistakably Captain Meredith – standing only a few yards from her. Uneasily she stayed where she was. Above, the fighters lunged, punched, stumbled, ducked, wrestled. She saw the Butcher's great hands get hold of Midnight's head, thumbs trying to gouge at his eyes. But Midnight was too quick. He twisted his head, stabbing his knuckles into the bulging gut, coming up as the man grunted and relaxed his grip, then seized the cauliflower ears, screwing them round, shoving the bald skull from him. He wasn't expecting Jem to collapse forward, feigning lost consciousness, his weight coming full force, taking both of them to the floor. The seconds moved in and the umpire began counting.

Heat and fright made Jess feel sick. One round and her legs were shaking, her nerves in rags. But they were getting up; going back to their corners. She told herself – he's all right. This is what we wanted anyway . . . what we worked for. But it was hard trying to convince herself.

Mat said in Midnight's ear: 'Surprise . . . surprise and speed. He didn't know what'd happened for a good two seconds in the first part of that round. It's the way through, lad. Slogging's no use. He's worth three o'thee at that game. Keep quick and keep him guessing. And look out for his right. When it connects, it's a killer.'

The words fell and locked in Midnight's brain as he moved into the chalk square for the next round. Bruised though his face was and the back of his head and ribs, his inner self felt fresh; energetic. The supreme confidence was still intact. There was no question that this was his fight, his day. He'd noticed Jem's laboured breathing. Heat, booze, age and too much flesh were telling. And he relied heavily on brute strength. Skill was but a small part of his game. Midnight caught sight of Jess. She was smiling and waving with both hands clasped together. He didn't return the smile. For the moment her importance was remote – a far-off diamond reward to be savoured when he was champion. He didn't think of James Lambert at all.

Inside the square he faced the white gorilla. The umpire's hand lowered. Immediately the heavy bulk launched towards him. He stepped to the right, hitting out with his left and his knuckles grazed Jem's rock fist, continuing on to his cheek. But the force was diminished. Another clumsy rush, which he avoided, moving back with such speed that the Butcher's second, who'd been shadow

175

fighting in empathy, got in the way. Midnight stumbled, almost fell, trying to twist away from Jem's murderous right fist, but not quite managing. He heard an explosion in his skull as an agonising pain shot through eyes, ears, nose – travelling over his head. He had wit enough to duck and retreat until his clouded senses cleared. A warm wet trickle of blood was running down his cheek. He rubbed it away, hearing Mat's voice in his mind.

'Surprise . . . surprise and speed . . .' Once before he'd floored this ox. He could do it again. Must do it.

The mob were howling advice and encouragement for anyone who would listen. The sight of blood raising the temperature of excitement. It triggered a fresh answering spurt of determination in Midnight, changing his cool confidence, which had wavered for the first time, into a warmer lust for success. It would, *must* come. He went back in.

The sight of blood running down Midnight's face was almost more than Jess could bear. All her earlier doubts came surging back to join fresh worries about his staying power. Good food and hard training had improved his fitness, but she knew that those long weeks of illness had taken their toll. He needed a quick knockout and she saw him try time and again. Once he brought Jem to his knees, only to be thrown himself seconds later. One round followed another. In an interval someone passed up a bottle of port for the fighters, but Midnight waved it on to Jem, accepting only a sip of water to refresh himself.

'Souse th'self, nigger. It'll hurt less when I smash thee,' Jem called through swollen lips.

'Don't take no heed,' Mat said, squeezing water over Midnight's head and neck, and wiping the oozing blood away.

Midnight shrugged, walking into the square. What did

words matter? They could only make the final success that much sweeter. But he knew his energy was less. He had to find his mark soon. They circled each other wearily. Then he moved in, taking a blow on his chest that half-halted him before he could placed his own punch, which landed hard but inaccurate. He heard Jess's voice for the first time as she cried out:

'Now . . . now . . .' rising to a pitch: 'NOW!'

With every ounce of his weight and strength he brought his right arm down in a swift killing blow. The shock of the impact of fist on jaw travelled in waves of pain up his arm. There was a heavy thud and the stage boards shuddered. A great cheer filled the air, and looking down he saw a mountain of white flesh heaving and rolling over at is feet.

He'd done it.

He looked for Jess to share his triumph. She was there, a small black and white shape against a spreading tide of men who weren't cheering, but were waving threatening arms. They pressed forward, crowding the stage, cursing and spitting. Jess vanished. He saw Mat yell something, but couldn't hear for the din. In a panic for her, he scrambled from the stage away from the angry miners. The friendly side of the crowd swallowed him up, patting him on the shoulders and head, telling him he was a great feller . . . a worthy champion. But these compliments, which would have been nectar before, he hardly heard as he pushed against the tide that moved inexorably towards the fairground; fighting back to find her. It was like the worst of his dreams when he swam with leaden arms in a sea of sucking mud. Just as he despaired, she came out from under the stage, pressing against him. She said:

'Christmas! This ain't no way to celebrate!' and then: 'Oh my stars . . . th'poor face!'

After that there was no breath for talking. They were

cramped together, helplessly moving as the crowd moved. Fights had broken out. There were shrieks and oaths and wails of alarm. A woman just in front of them fainted, but couldn't fall and was swept along, crushed ever tighter as the mob overflowed into the fairground. There, individual fights joined up into an exuberant brawl that increased and overturned several stalls. Apples, carrots, pins, plates, beads, ribbons, crocks, glass went hurling into the melting-pot of heaving waving arms and legs. Even the gingerbread men weren't spared. Mongrels and urchins nippy enough had a feast. But Jess and Midnight weren't concerned with scavenging. Ribs on the point of cracking, they were suddenly spewed into a looser brawl and were greeted with shouts of:

'Here's our champion! He's come to lend a hand. He'll sort out the men from the boys . . .' People surged round and Midnight waved his hands in refusal.

'No more fighting today, my friends!' He put his arms protectively round Jess, meaning to guide her to a narrow gap between the actor's booth and a barrow of oranges. But it closed before their eyes. A gang of youths coming out of a nearby bush house to join in the fun, saw and swooped. Oranges rained down like vast hailstones.

'Lord save us . . . can't we get out?' Jess gasped.

'We'll get thee out . . . don't th'fret, love . . . come on lads . . .' Midnight's supporters turned on the youths who reacted first with a barrage of oranges then, seeing they were outnumbered, took to their heels. There were shouts of glee, while underfoot the trodden oranges squelched and made mud of the dust. One or two supporters went down, cursing amid laughter.

But there were other shouts, less friendly. Jess glanced round and saw again the Captain's white face. He was shouldering towards them, accompanied by some tough-looking seaman. She heard his voice commanding:

'Get that nigger!'

Midnight had also heard and seen, but the seamen, daunted by the growing number of admirers who swarmed around him, turned away. Pushed back by the crowd, the Captain stood no chance, as more and more people left the miners and the fights, eager for closer contact with this man who had managed to vanquish the great Butcher Jem. They pressed in and Jess said desperately:

'Lordy . . . now we're trapped good and true!'

Midnight appealed to the crowd: 'Friends, you'll understand me when I say I need drink and rest. Make way for us!'

The word went round. 'Let un out . . . Make room . . . Give un a shoulder lift . . . Look after the lass . . .'

There was no holding them back, and alarmed and thrilled, Jess saw Midnight seized, lifted high, then carried forward. He looked back at her, anxious, elated, bewildered. Infected by the jaunty mood around her she smiled her delight and encouragement, following close behind. She was protected now by the core of the crowd that stayed faithful, while the outer rim fluctuated and dropped away, leaving a small band of cheering enthusiasts to process through the holiday streets back to the Hatchett Inn.

Mat and Randall were waiting, in equally good mood.

'I was worried about thee, lad,' Mat said, as Midnight was deposited on the floor of the tap-room. 'What in the name of Satan made thee fight the crowd? Th'should have gone with 'em.'

'I went back for Jess,' Midnight said.

Mat frowned slightly and Randall said: 'Women are men's delight and downfall . . . but no more of a hazard than that unreasonable mob. Mayhem. Lunacy and mayhem!'

shook his head, then giving Midnight's shoulder a light tap added: 'But all's well . . . and here you are shirtless, begrimed and without your prize! I can at least remedy one of those misfortunes.' He held out a small leather bag.

Midnight took it with a brief nod of thanks, opened it and carefully counted the fifteen gold coins. For a moment he looked at them lying in his open palm then, slipping them back in the bag, secured the strings and tucked it in the broad belt at his waist. Jess was expecting him to show his pleasure, but he didn't and she was left puzzled and slightly disappointed.

'That should keep thee in port and brandy for a while,' someone called.

'It's ale that he wants right now,' Mat said handing Midnight a tankard of frothing beer. 'Here's to thee! And thee . . .' supplying Jess with the same.

She took it and drunk deep, disappointment dispelled by the triumph and enjoyment of the moment.

Fifteen

July had given way to August and Midnight had fought and won two more contests. His fame was gradually spreading and Jess was delighted. In the Hatchett tap-room she served a one-eyed man with beer, took his money and dropped it into the cracked jug with the rest of the takings, only half aware of what she was doing. Her mind was full of last week's fight and the glorious cheering moment when Daniel Kelly, the burly Irish sailor, had fallen like a stone. Midnight had got a lump on his face as big as an apple doing it, but the ten-guinea purse made up for that! She looked down at the ring on her finger. A little gold ring in the shape of a snake, tail in its mouth and a tiny green stone eye; bought from a peddler that same night. There'd been a host of pretty gewgaws on his tray, but none she'd fancied as much.

'It's yours if you like it,' Midnight had said and bought it for her.

She smiled to herself, remembering the delight, and how the peddler had stared at first, then winked. He wasn't the only one to stare at them. Sometimes she was astonished herself. Never in all her life had she thought she'd be a blackamoor's wench. She'd scarcely imagined ever being anyone's wench! The whole thing was an astonishment from beginning to end. From the beginning anyway. Ends didn't come into it; not yet ... not for a long time ... perhaps not ever. For the moment he was her love and she wished with all her heart she could go out to the stable this very minute and hug him – to make up for being so sharp that morning. But the customers had to be served and the horses tended. Time together was pared down to the bone, and that was the trouble. Her temper got frayed and she said things she didn't mean. That very morning her tongue had run off with her over nothing at all. He'd been slow in answering Mat's suggestion of a return match with Butcher Jem. A long silence, then he'd said:

'Perhaps.' That was all.

'Th'd be a fool to turn it down,' she'd said.

'Perhaps,' again.

'Perhaps . . . perhaps . . . oh!' and she'd banged about with plates and mugs. Not that it helped. He'd gone on sitting there all shut in, and that's when the lying waspish words slipped out.

'What's the matter – doubt th'chances next time?'

He'd spoken then, and as sharp: 'Shallow thinking! There's more to life than fighting,' with a look that had told her she was being a fool.

The shame came back, and she looked down at the ring again. It was her very first present and so beautiful she couldn't keep her eyes off it. She'd make it up to him. As if to put herself into this mood, she gave herself a little shake and began collecting empty tankards, whisking away from the venturesome hands of a tipsy man with a nose like a beacon and a wig that looked as if it had satisfied the appetites of a family of moths. She deposited the tankards on a tray, held it up for Mrs Mat to see, nodding towards the door as she did so, then went out to wash them in the kitchen. Surprisingly it was empty. The temptation to snatch a few minutes with Midnight was too great to resist. She put the tray on the table and went across the yard.

He was in the stable feeding and watering a stocky

brown cob, and glanced up, hearing her step. There was a wary look about him which was a silent reproach and, stupidly, made her less ready to say she was sorry for her bad temper. He broke the awkward silence by saying:

'Won't you be missed in the tap-room?'

She put her nose in the air. 'They can do without me for two minutes. I works like a slave most of the time.' It wasn't the happiest choice of words, but it said what she felt, and brought a slight smile to his face.

'You do,' he said. 'As for me, the work is less fraught with threat, but carries its own troubles.' He took a strong brush from a rack on the wall and began cleaning the dusty coat of a roan mare standing in the stall next to the cob.

She watched, puzzled by what he'd said, trying to work out the meaning without having to ask; still suffering from a reluctant tongue, though she really did want to put things right.

He went on brushing the mare with long steady strokes in the rhythmical way he did everything. 'There's pleasure in this work. It brings me calm and a quiet spirit, unlike so much else.' He looked up and smiled hesitantly, without stopping what he was doing. 'There are moments when my bondage is more than I can peaceably bear. I'm sorry.'

All her reluctance was washed away and she went and put her arms round his neck, her cheek on the back of his shoulder. 'It's me as should say sorry. I get that crotchety some days. There's no time!'

He didn't say anything, but briefly put his large hand over hers; then returned to brushing the mare. She let go, less demonstrative now that things between them had slotted back into place, but a lingering doubt stayed with her. What did he mean – his bondage? There didn't seem any answer and she repeated: 'No time,' sighing.

'They steal it from us. We can't do what we would,' he

said, startling her even more when he added: 'I feel a growing disgust with my life . . .'

'But th'bist free,' she interrupted. 'Don't th'recall what th'said? About dignity and not being a slave . . . being equal, th'said.' They were his words, his beliefs, not hers. All along she thought he didn't see things quite straight and it made him want what he could never have. But being disgusted . . . there was no sense to it.

'Three fights can alter false beliefs,' he said and this time he gave her all his attention, leaving the horse.

'False? Th'weren't in the wrong. A bit of a green lad, but not wrong!' She felt suddenly much older than her seventeen years, older than him, and arguing for the beliefs she'd doubted before, seemed perfectly sensible.

He came close. 'I am an animal to those crowds. A clever punching brute who can give them excitement through violence. Popular only because I can hit harder and with better result than other men. *They don't know my mind.*'

She didn't know what to make of this and said: 'What's that got to do with being a prizefighter?'

'You cup the answer in your hands,' he said, making even less sense.

She held up her hands and saw the green stone eye sparkle; feeling as if she was listening with muffled ears. Not for the first time she knew she was out of her depth. Everything that had been clear – winning the prizefights, enjoying the good times the money brought – grew misty. The sensation was unnerving. She wanted him to go on talking so that she might get a chance of understanding without having to ask for explanations, but again there was no time.

Mat's voice bellowed: 'Jess . . . Jess . . . where the bloody hell are th'hiding!' They heard him stumping across the yard and Jess said under her breath:

''Tis allus the same . . . do this . . . do that . . .' coming out of the warm sticky hay-scented shadows into the florid brightness to face an irritated Mat who said:

'Th've no business going to the stables when th'should be serving. I don't employ thee to kiss and cuddle. And where's Midnight? MIDNIGHT . . .'

Jess didn't wait, but scuttled back into the kitchen, washed the tankards at a great rate, then swept them back into the tap-room – the old fear of being put on the streets dogging her heels. She was surprised when Midnight came in with Mat seconds later. They went to the table under the window where a young man in neat dark clothes was sitting. He moved his head, and Jess saw his profile sharp against the light. She recognised him immediately as the man on the horse they had met down at the waterfront. Now what in the world did he want with Midnight? She tried to watch and listen, but there were customers to be served and the hum of conversation and the scrape of feet and tankards clinking and occasional laughter – all there specially to hinder and infuriate her.

At the table Mat said: 'This is Midnight, sir.'

The man smiled. 'I'm glad to make your acquaintance. Your fame spreads wide. I'm Thomas Clarkson . . . but we have met before, surely?'

'By the river. On Broad Quay,' Midnight said.

'I remember of course. You directed me to the Friends' Meeting House. Please sit down and partake of some refreshment. A tankard of beer for you?'

Midnight looked surprised, but nodded, saying: 'I thank you,' accepting a place on the settle opposite. He knew Mat was taken aback and saw him go off and say something to Jess, who brought the beer. He took it, nodding thanks again gravely, avoiding her searching look, her reluctant retreat, knowing she was eaten up by curiosity. He felt a certain mildly suspicious interest himself and waited to hear why he'd been summoned.

'I'm in Bristol on a mission concerning the abolition of the slave trade,' Thomas Clarkson said, coming straight to the point. 'To pursue this goal I need information – any information – about the nature of the trade. Any events of note. Any details of sea life. Any histories of ill-treatment of slaves or seamen.' He paused with an expectant look, but Midnight remained impassive. Clarkson went on: 'I'm working under the patronage of Mr Wilberforce – a gentleman of great influence in Parliamentary circles and a good friend of the Prime Minister . . . indeed Mr Pitt is himself drawn to our Cause. I understand this may mean little to you, but I want you to realise that we are not dealing here in idle curiosity. We are determined to use all information as a weapon in our fight for the total abolition of slavery.'

There was sincerity in his voice, but there had been sincerity in John Sanderson's voice when he had said: 'I abhor the practice of flogging slaves,' leaving Gomer free to whip and whip again behind the sugar canes.

'Why do you come to me?' Midnight asked.

'Because you have suffered the indignity of being a slave. If you would, I am sure you could tell me much that would assist my study.'

Midnight drank some of the beer, taking his time so that he could think. He was surprised by the request and not yet ready to believe in the honesty of this white stranger. The response in himself, the flooding desire to give every aid to help wipe out the abomination, alarmed him. It came with passionate abandon. He dared not respond without further thought. There were too many pitfalls; too many traps.

'Well?'

'It is true I was once a slave, but now I am a free man.'

'John Dean was a free man. You know John Dean?'

Hot pitch on his back and the tongs tearing at his flesh while he was pinned helpless as a stuck pig to the deck. Oh yes, he knew of John Dean! The free nigger! So did Captain Meredith. He had plucked the tale and kept it for his own, experimenting in much the same way with the poor wretch Billy Waring.

'I have heard of the man,' he admitted slowly.

Clarkson leaned forward. 'He was supposedly a free man also.' He paused as if to let the weight of his words sink in fully, then went on: 'I've tried to contact him. Mr Donovan, the landlord at his old lodgings, had told all he could, but the man himself has removed to London. A free man! No more a slave! You see my studies have taught me already that once a vessel sails on the vile triangular voyage, crew and cargo are lumped together in miserable servitude. It must cease. It must be fought with never ending concentration until it is obliterated. But to do it, there must be fact, and fact on paper.'

In his mind, Midnight heard the strange Englishwoman, Miss Jarman, making a similar claim for the importance of fact, but for very different reasons. It was an irony of mountainous proportion. He repeated very quietly to himself: 'The fact is, slavery is the backbone of Bristol.'

'What's that?'

'Only some words I once heard spoken by the owner of such a vessel. "Slavery is the backbone of Bristol" – as such it will go hard with you if you try to kill it.'

'Nothing is won without risk. And there is much dislike of the trade. Much talk against it, but . . .'

'But little written fact?' Midnight supplied.

Clarkson laughed. 'I produce my pen and paper, and

what happens? My informers have urgent business elsewhere, or a bad attack of cramp in the hand, or can't sign their name because they have never learned to write; can't even hold a pen well enough to make a cross!'

'I write a bold hand,' Midnight said, his passion overriding his caution.

'You speak fluently also. Does that mean you will give me help?'

Midnight answered with a question: 'Who told you of me?'

'Your own fame and Mr Thompson of the Seven Stars. He has given me much aid, taking me to the hells of Marsh Street night after night; putting me in contact with sailors and Captains alike. He spoke of your arrival with a certain Captain Meredith. And the rumours about him were enough to make me wish to seek you out.'

'The Captain is already in trouble with the law – for fraud,' Midnight said, quietly bitter.

'I had heard, though the case hangs fire.'

Midnight looked up from studying the wet beer rings on the table. 'For what reason?'

'I believe the chief witness has disappeared. Mr Thompson also mentioned something about the illness of the plaintiff.' Clarkson eyed him shrewdly. 'Perhaps you have evidence that will be sought.'

'I have no interest in fraud.'

'You protect him then? He was perhaps easy with crew and prisoners, and I have been misled.'

The screws were biting intolerably into the base of his thumb nails. Squeezing. Tightening until blood spurted from his thumb ends. Pain shrieked along arms, neck, head and out through his voice. He heard it again, while the white devil smiled and listened and enjoyed.

Oh God have mercy . . . On and on. Mercy . . . mercy
. . . mercy . . .

From a great distance a voice said: 'You disagree?'
Midnight looked down at his hands gripping the pewter
tankard and saw his thumbs slim and uncrushed, the nails
thickening and ridged at the quick. He let go and
examined his palms without replying, while a few flies
knocked helplessly against the diamond window-panes
and smoke from clay pipes spiralled and spread in a thin
blue cloud. He knew that Mat was hovering in the
background and Jess was keeping up an endless stream of
rapid glances. Both were on pins to learn of what had been
spoken. Yet still he could not finally make up his mind.

'I need more time,' he said at last. 'If you are what you
claim and your interest has the strength of which you
speak, then you will understand that cruel experience has
instructed me in caution.'

Clarkson sighed and drank in the last of his beer.
'Perhaps you may reconsider . . .' He let the last sentence
drift away on a question.

'I will. One thing I promise – to come to you again and
tell you my decision.' Midnight put out his hand and
Clarkson took it, shaking it vigorously.

'A bargain, my friend.'

The genuine warmth of the handshake and the
piercingly honest gaze acted on Midnight like the releasing
of a long-coiled spring. He almost broke his own decision
there and then, and told all he knew, but managed to hold
back, signalling to Jess, who skipped between the tables
with the agility of a dancer.

'You will drink a pint with me this time?' he asked.

'Surely. I am obliged to you.'

Bringing the beer, Jess felt like pouring it over the pair

of them, her curiosity steaming away with no hope of it being quenched for hours to come. She had to contain herself until nightfall and some stolen moments in the hayloft when the questions came pouring out.

'He is seeking my history . . . asking for information that is against the trade in slaves,' Midnight said when he could get a word in.

Jess was instantly suspicious. 'Why? What do he want from thee?'

'I've told you.'

'No, but what really?'

'He speaks honestly. It is evident in his voice and manner. He loathes slaving nearly as I loathe it.' He was certain of this truth as he spoke, and knew that he would help.

'What folks say and what they mean ain't allus the same,' Jess said. 'Th'don't want to stir up a hornet's nest. Th'might get stung.'

He knew she could be right and put his arms round her as they lay together. 'I must do it.'

She pulled back from him, still uneasy. 'Slavery's behind thee and the future's bright. Th'don't want to do aught as 'ud spoil th'chances.' A worry like a tapeworm had been gnawing at her all day. She had to know if she'd understood him aright.

He was silent for a minute, looking over he shoulder, not at the mound of hay or the wall or the window, but some distant thing she couldn't fathom and again she felt miserably cut off.

'I have this thought in my mind . . . this conviction . . .' he began and paused, coming back from his distances to look at her intently. 'We seek happiness, all of us – you know that, don't you?'

She was aware that he was trying to pick out words and

put them together simply, so she would understand. Swamped by his gaze and her own sense of inadequacy, she felt as if she was getting smaller and smaller. She nodded, but in a bid to save herself, said brusquely:

"Course I do. Everyone does . . . if they're lucky enough to have time to think.'

'We have time. Not much, but enough for thought. And there is no happiness for me in prizefighting. I've tried to explain how it . . . diminishes what I am. Say you understand!' He made the appeal and the tone of his voice was clear if not his words. She hung on to him; fearful of what seemed to be happening; angry because there was a large part of him she didn't understand and suspected she never would; wanting to make him see things as she did.

'Ain't this happiness, being together – not just loving with our bodies, but . . . but . . .' defeated, she lay still, burying her head in his chest.

'Yes. I would not deny that – not for the whole world.'

She could hear great tenderness side by side with a tinge of exasperation.

'But there is much more . . . so much more.' He abandoned any attempt at manipulating his words. 'There is only one way for me. I must go home!' It was out. The dream he'd been harbouring for months; years. He looked at her eagerly. 'Say you will come with me back to my country. I've money now, not enough to buy passages for us both yet, but I will fight for more. I'll fight Butcher Jem . . . and win!' The last with a touch of humour, but Jess didn't notice. The loft seemed to be parting company with itself, brick from brick, boards floating away, the roof sailing off into space leaving her adrift nowhere.

'*Africa!*' He might just as well have asked her to go visiting the stars.

'Yes – back to the Eboes, my brothers.'

'But th'said they were killed or taken for slaves.'

'Some must still be there. I will search till I find them.'

'And if th'don't?'

'I'll start the tribe all over again.'

She almost spoke out then and told him, but the words got lost, and when she did speak, said: 'With me?' to test his reaction.

He was silent. She knew her point had gone home and she was answered. The awfulness lay not only here, but in the way he'd apparently thrown their careful plans overboard. Silence pressed down until she could bear it no longer.

'What else did that Mr Clarkson say?' she asked.

'Oh, news about the court case. It would seem James Lambert has vanished, and Miss Jarman being ill, all is at a standstill.'

Jess was startled. A vague sense of guilt that she'd thought dead, reared up, though why she should feel guilty (except for stealing that shilling and sixpence) was a mystery. She asked: 'What be wrong with her?'

'I have no knowledge. He said merely that the plaintiff is ill.'

'Oh . . . that could be Lawyer Loveitt then,' Jess said, only half believing.

'Perhaps . . . who is to say?' He answered absently. Solitude occupied all of him and could not be dislodged even though he tightened his hold on Jess.

'I'll go and find out,' she said, muffled against his chest and by the struggle she was having to hold back resentful tears. 'I'll go tomorrow. Mrs Mat'll surely give me time off on a Sunday.'

Midnight said nothing, striving to close the gap between them with caresses as words seemed useless. He felt her respond and tasted the tears on her cheeks. A little hope came back, but not enough to heal.

Sixteen

It was two Sundays before Jess was able to get time off to visit Miss Phoebe as she said she would. Walking up the hill towards Jarman House was toilsome and she felt weary. It was the sickness, she told herself. She'd spewed twice that morning, and with the hot sun as well it was enough to flatten anyone, however tough. But deep down was a niggling feeling that the tiredness stemmed from the way life had altered. There was an ever-developing stress between herself and Midnight. It was hard putting a finger on just exactly what had come to separate them. Things being the way they were, they ought to be growing closer together. Not that they quarrelled. It was more of an invisible wall with Midnight on one side and herself on the other. Perhaps it was her fault. Perhaps she should speak out, but a strange reluctance tied her tongue. She sighed and rubbed her tender stomach, giving up thinking in favour of looking about her.

There was a richness in the dusty ripened leaves thick on summer trees, and a sweet scent that must be coming from the flowers she'd glimpsed in the gardens behind private walls. Sunday silence was very settled; hardly disturbed by the smooth drone of bees and the small bird gossip. The peace of it was a treat after the clatter and rush of the inn. Over the separating weeks she'd forgotten how much she'd enjoyed those rare tastes of being alone.

A beech tree. A length of rosy brick wall. Sagging iron

gates. More wall . . . and there was the familiar tradesman's door – plain wood, the paint blistered and faded to dull greeny-blue – opening into the concealed path. It occurred to her suddenly that the old baggages couldn't have done so well out of the slaving business, or the property would be in better trim. Not that it mattered to her. She was no part of their life any more.

She opened the door, went inside and closed herself into the secret world of trees and shrubs and time. Not her world, she reminded herself briskly, and rummaging under her skirt found the hanging pocket and took out her debt. She was not going to stay. A quick word of explanation to Miss Phoebe and an inquiry as to the health of the old cow, then home.

Home!

The word had sneaked into her mind in the meanest way, making her whole body feel limp with a ragbag of longing, dreams, hope – none of which had a definite shape, but left her queasy again. It wouldn't do! She couldn't spew a third time . . . not here! In a sweat of anxiety she almost ran up the rest of the path, going through the archway towards the kitchen door.

'Stars above . . . look who's here!' Sally Dade said. 'Th've chosen a fine time to visit and no mistake. Don't stand on the doorstep. Come in . . . come in. Th'looks right peaked.'

Jess went into the kitchen and at Sally's bidding sat on a chair half-mesmerised by the babbled questions.

'I've heard such tales about thee and that nigger. He's a big strapping feller ain't he? I went to his last fight and it were grand the way he floored that Irish feller. Tell us, is it true th'bist going with un? And is he good to thee? That's a pretty ring . . . go on, show us . . . was it a present?'

'Yes,' Jess managed to squeeze in, taking hold of the

opportunity to ask: 'Is Miss Phoebe at home? It's her I've come to see.'

The door to the passage opened rapidly before Sally could answer, and Salt limped in. When she saw Jess, she registered surprise and annoyance, then closing the door with unexpected gentleness, said briskly: 'There ain' no work for such as thee, if that's what the've come for.'

'I ain't,' Jess said, relieved rather than annoyed by the familiar attack. 'I've come on private business to see Miss Phoebe.'

'Then th'should choose thy calling day more careful. Miss Phoebe's not got time nor feeling for listening to kitchen wenches as take themselves off without even a by th'leave! And if she had – kind soul as she is – now's not the time, when she's bothered to death with all the arrangements as need seeing to.'

'Arrangements?'

'For the funeral. Didn't th'know? Miss Jarman was took the day afore yesterday and is to be buried tomorrow – God rest her soul!' There was a croakiness about Salt's voice that startled Jess almost more than the news. She put a calloused bony hand to her eye, quickly rubbing it as she sniffed and turned away to busy herself at the fire.

Jess looked at Sally who said: ''Tis true. She got a fit of the apoplexy three weeks back. Been like a helpless babby ever since. Couldn't move, couldn't say aught. Lying there with her face all twisted up . . .'

'Stop th'chattering, will thee! Gabble, gabble from morn till night.' Salt turned round, dry-eyed now and fiercely red. 'The parlour dust sheets can come off and the rugs rolled ready for beating. Look sharp about it.'

'On Sunday?' Sally protested.

'When I tellee, that's when. There's not to be one speck o'dust come tomorrow.' Salt's voice, never quiet, had expanded to reach the kitchen walls and beyond. Jess couldn't help a smile in spite of the jolt of Miss Jarman's death, but it faded quickly. The old cow gone! An unexpected ache took her by surprise. She saw Sally bounce towards the door, pulling a face and winking, then going beetroot red as she came face to face with Miss Phoebe on her way in.

'Jess!' Miss Phoebe said.

The grey pock-marked face, the puffy eyes red-rimmed, the untidy black dress that hadn't seen a flat iron since it came out of mothballs, above all the hint of pleasure in the tired watery smile, swelled the ache and made Jess temporarily forget all about why she'd come. She said impulsively:

'I'm that sorry, miss. I didn't know till now. She were good to me.' Not that knowing or saying anything made a farthing of difference, but she did care and what other way was there to show it?

'Oh . . . yes . . . thank you.'

No questions. No frowns or sharp questions about why she ran off. Nothing but the smile that grew more and more watery. There was so much more Jess wanted to say, but the right words wouldn't come into her mind.

'She's going, Miss Phoebe.' Salt glared at Jess.

'There's no need on my account,' Miss Phoebe said in a gentle vague way.

Pity touched Jess. She felt again the pull of the old bond and wondered if there was any similar feeling in return. It seemed unlikely. She got up from the chair, meaning to go, and became aware of the money, warm and sticky in her hand.

'I came to pay back me owings, miss,' she said, going across and holding it out.

'Owings? I can't recollect . . .' Miss Phoebe began

fidgeting with the bits of lace at her neck. Her habitual worried look come back, and Jess said hastily:

'The money for th'cap ribbons. Th'new cap that were made for the Frolic.' She stopped as quickly as she had begun. Admitting the truth wasn't as easy as she'd expected. She was risking real trouble if she said she'd stolen it. 'I took it because . . . because . . .' She was being as hesitant as the old woman in front of her. 'Because I had need of a loan, as I were being pressed to pay . . . a debt.' Ashamed and relieved, she blew out her cheeks.

Miss Phoebe looked more bewildered than ever.

'Th've no right to bother Miss Phoebe with such things. Th'deserve a good hiding, and I'd give it to thee meself if I hadn't better things to do,' Salt scolded. 'Now be off with thee!'

Miss Phoebe had been listening in a dazed fashion. Now she looked back at Jess, who was still holding out the money not knowing quite what to do with it.

'It's good of you, dear,' she murmured. 'I'm glad to find my trust wasn't misplaced.'

Salt made a sound of disgust, something between a cough and a snort, but Jess didn't care twopence for anything she might think. The importance lay in Miss Phoebe's words, and the way she took the money, briefly squeezing the hand that offered it.

'I came down for something . . .' The small contact seemed to have muddled her even more. 'What was it?'

'Summat about the . . . arrangements?' Jess suggested diffidently.

'No. It was . . . oh yes. A tray of tea. I was thirsty.'

Not thirsty . . . lonely – Jess thought. Again she spoke impulsively:

'I'll make thee one, miss, and bring it up.' It was the least she could do.

'Thank you . . . so nice . . . Mrs Salt is overburdened with all the extra . . .' Miss Phoebe went to the door and hesitated with her hand on the knob. 'See that there are two dishes,' she said. 'We'll take it in the morning-room.'

'Well!' Salt exclaimed as she closed the door. 'Well . . .'

Jess didn't know what to think. Had the old baggage gone off her head, ordering for two; talking of 'we' as if her sister was still alive? She seemed confused, though not witless.

'Woolgathering?' Salt asked. 'The kettle's steaming and th'knows where the china is, so get on with it.'

In a curious way everything had dropped back, as if time had taken a tuck in itself and she'd never left. A strange feeling that made laying the tray and filling the teapot dreamlike. The truth was that everything had changed. Miss Jarman was dead, while she, Jess, had grown up.

She picked up the tray and went into the passage and up the stairs into the morning-room, where the sun had faded the striped wallpaper to yellow-cream and dusty rose, bringing the growing sense of dream with her.

'Put it on the table, my dear.' Miss Phoebe seemed more in command, sitting in her usual tapestry chair. 'That's right. And when you've poured tea for us both, draw up a seat. I want to hear of your life since you left us. Everything. Forgive an old woman's curiosity, but I have a need to . . . busy myself.'

Astounded, Jess did what she was asked, as the real world moved further and further away; sitting down on the very edge of the small ribbon-back chair. Awkward at first, then growing easier, with the halting words becoming fluent. Telling everything – except the closely guarded secret of the baby she carried.

Midnight scanned the long sheets of paper, examining his bold script for any inaccuracies of content or spelling.

. . . these Wooden Yokes were placed round our necks and in this manner were forced to walk until we reached the sea . . .

. . . brought on deck to stretched our cramped limbs, being then flogged until we hopped and stumbled in a Grotesk Dance. No one was spared. Even those lowered by the Flux did not escape . . .

. . . determined to bring my Unhappy Life to an end by refusing to eat or drink. I did not know of the terrible instrument Speculum Oris when taking my Decision. I quickly learned when the Surgeon forced this Weapon of Torture between my clenched Teeth, breaking one of them and poking the back of my Tongue until I thought I must choke to death. He then proceeded to screw open my mouth ready for the Vile Concoction which was at hand to pour in . . .

. . . horror filled me. Some of the Women in their Terror tried to scale the wooden surround of the Market Place, but were dragged back. One Man did escape and was pursued through the Town. I know not what became of him. The Overseer, whom I then imagined to be my Master as he had bought me, shackled us together and drove us out into the street . . .

. . . from sunrise to sunset we laboured, severing the tough canes, the stubble cutting our legs and feet, the lash our only Music . . .

. . . lived in miserable Shacks constructed by ourselves, with no bed but the mud floor and a single threadbare Blanket for warmth. Food was often tainted, but even so there were many Rats who wished to partake of our Repast . . .

. . . an old white-haired man who said his name was Jacob. We conversed and I learned he was Personal Slave to Mr John Sanderson. That was my first understanding of Gomer's true position. Until then I had regarded *him* as my owner as he had traded for me. Afterwards . . .

. . . chosen for my strength in the first instance. Mr Sanderson had difficulty in moving and I had to lift him from his Chair and his Bed. Later, observing my quickness in acquiring the English Language, he decided I should be successor to Jacob as Amanuensis and Reader. Therefore did I learn much of Literature . . .

. . . with the Summer of 1784 came my first Encounter with the seafaring Captain, Abel Meredith, when he came as guest to my Master . . .

. . . tried to bargain for me. Offering Thirty Five Guineas, he said he would have me . . .

. . . informed Captain Meredith that the Slave Bettina was not for sale, neither was she for his personal use, but he could choose any other Female he so desired. At this the Captain was incensed as he did not take well to having his wishes balked . . .

. . . knew nothing of the suggested purchase of the Plantation. Then came the sad day when my Master died. His son, Henry, had already left Montserrat and wished only for a Speedy Sale. Captain Meredith was the purchaser . . .

Midnight dipped his quill in the ink, examined it, then continued writing.

. . . Mr Lascar boarded the *Princess* late one night as we lay at anchor in the Port of Spanish Town . . . utmost secrecy . . . being Slave I was regarded as part of the Cabin Furnishings, no more an ear than the Table of Lanthorn.

Thus I learned that Mr Lascar in his lack of wisdom had discovered to Captain Meredith of the aforementioned fraud. In a bid to prevent betrayal to the Insurance Company, the Owners of the Princess and the Guardians of the English Law, he was offered an equal share in the Plantation. The Bargain was sealed, but not honoured. On a foggy day as we lay becalmed off the Coast of Cornwall I witnessed the still Living Body of Mr John Lascar thrown into the sea. Death had not come although he had been Stabbed, of that I swear. The Man who threw him overboard was Captain Abel Meredith . . .

. . . flogged me with no regard for my position as a Free Man . . .

. . . all this I affirm to be true and do this Day the Twenty First of August 1787 put my Hand to – signing with both Real and Slave names.

He let out a long slow breath and, refilling the quill, wrote below:

Olaudah, of the Tribe of Eboe.

and underneath:

Midnight

Putting down the quill, he sanded the wet ink before handing the paper to Thomas Clarkson, who, with Landlord Thompson, was waiting to witness it.

The business complete, Clarkson shook Midnight's hand warmly. 'I cannot thank you enough. This information is invaluable . . . invaluable.'

'Should cook the Cap'n's goose!' Thompson said, smiling until his face looked ready to split in two. 'I knew he were a right bad lot as soon as I clapped eyes on him. "Meredith's Law" indeed!' He spat on the floor.

'His days are numbered,' Clarkson said. 'No court of law could possibly acquit him.'

Well aware that things might be very different if Mr John Lascar had been a nigger, Midnight said crisply: 'In my opinion his greater crimes lie in his cruelty to his innocent human cargoes.'

Clarkson looked up from reading over the account. 'I don't dispute that. Don't ever think I would dispute it.' There could be no doubting that he meant every word. A quiet unshakable integrity was in everything he did. Midnight was reassured. He put his hand to his neck.

'It is difficult. The collar is gone, but suspicion and distrust are less easy to remove.'

Thompson said with great feeling: 'Ah it's a bad business. Would to God us Bristol folk had steered clear of it. We need a few more long-sighted uns like them as owns the *Emerald*. I were talking to Cap'n Daws only the other day – he's her Master – and he were telling me he's taking her on the Triangular run with a difference. There's to be no trade in slaves. Instead he's out for stuff as is welcome in the Indies as well as here . . . things like gum-opal, palm oil, Cayenne pepper, ivory, woods of different sorts . . .'

'It's what I've always striven to make you understood,' Clarkson broke in eagerly. There's no *need* to barter for human beings. Honest trade with Africa can bring just as much wealth. Captain Daws, did you say? Where may I contact him?'

'Well now, I don't know whether th'will find him aboard – the *Emerald*'s at anchor in the Kingroad. Or he might still be lodging at the Galleon.'

Jolted out of his thoughts, Midnight looked across at Thompson. He stood up and Clarkson interrupted his conversation to say: 'You are leaving?'

Midnight inclined his head. 'In England free men must work.' He allowed himself to smile, feeling again the spontaneous joy and relief at having struck a blow at slavery. A responsive smile lightened the face of the grave Englishman. Midnight's hand was gripped and shaken twice in succession before he was able to escape.

The walk from the Seven Stars to the Galleon was long enough to give him time to think about the idea already taking shape in his mind. The success of it depended on whether or not the *Emerald* was already fully manned.

He quickened his footsteps. The longing to return home was like a huge thirst pursuing him day and night. This chance, so rare, so real, so elusive, must work! And in changing dreams to fact surely Jess would be persuaded to come with him? He so wanted to introduce her to his land, his people. The ghost of the old mistrust, the old feeling they were strangers came gliding back. He firmly set them aside along with the memory of her question 'With me?' and his terrible answering silence, which said as clearly as if he'd spoken the words 'Any child of ours could not be accepted into my tribe.' He'd almost been guilty of the same cruel prejudice he abhorred in the white masters, who used their slave women but rejected any bastard children fathered by them. Shame reared up, and coming to the Stone Bridge he paused to look and listen, hoping to rid himself of the twilight foreboding that was his constant companion.

The rash of vessels stretched out of sight inland. River life, even on a Sunday, was richly scented and busy. Men worked and idled. He heard the lap of water, the creak of floating timber, the flap of loose wind-blown sails. It brought strong revulsion and sweet longing combined. He must succeed. Against all odds, he *must*.

He began walking again; long strides that covered the distance rapidly, reaching the turn into the side street to find the inn sign – a galleon in full sail – squeaking backwards and forwards in the dusty wind. The door was open and he went inside, turning left into the cramped tap-room that was warm and fuggy and ripe with the smell of ale and people. He looked round for someone who might match the description of Captain Daws. There were several seaman no more than ordinary deckhands; an elderly man with white whiskers and a goitrous neck by the window, and another, thin and clerkish, sitting opposite. Still searching, he turned and found himself within spitting distance of Captain Meredith, who had just come through the doorway.

Midnight felt an instinctive prickle of fear which made him angry. He saw the Captain hesitate, trembling as he struggled to hold down his monstrous anger. The pale burning gaze scanned the room, returning to rest on him. Midnight watched, lynx eyed; wary and untrusting. Amongst all these people nothing could happen, but still he would not take any chance.

The Captain came closer, letting out a long slow breath like the subsiding of organ bellows. His voice came, a low hoarse undertone, on the tail of it: 'Animal – loathsome animal!' Without turning his head he continued to search the room with rapid nervous movements of his eyes. 'You are condemned!'

Midnight stood rock still, forcing himself to speak calmly: 'I come here on private business. I have no wish to speak to you.'

'Private business indeed! Ape. I have business with you, but not here. Business I will settle at the moment I choose.'

'Whatever that business may be, it is no longer a concern of mine,' Midnight replied. He suddenly felt a strange sense of total command. He looked straight at the Captain. 'I wonder you are still here. Don't you realise your powers have gone? You are in grave danger.'

He saw the face contort with scarcely contained fury.

'You dare to mention that. Treacherous filth. I know all of your lies, your falsehoods. Loveitt told me all you said. But never think I can be diverted by such as you from claiming my kingdom, I tell you . . .'

But he was interrupted by a shout from across the room: 'Hey . . . Midnight! Have some ale with us, shipmate. We owe thee summat for beating the Irishman.' One of the seamen, a stocky man with marvellous tattoos of a ship and mermaid on each of his arms, had left his table and was coming towards them. He clapped a gnarled hand on Midnight's shoulder. 'Won me two guineas th'did.'

The Captain stared as if he would shrivel him, but the man had attention only for Midnight. He turned away, beckoning the landlord, calling for more ale, and in that brief second the Captain said under his breath: 'You haven't heard the last of this affair, or of me,' a great depth of hatred in his voice. But Midnight knew now that the threatening words were impotent; no more than empty husks. He smiled and said:

'The whole world has heard the last of you and I know you have heard the last of me.'

The seaman had turned back, catching some of the words. 'Trouble, shipmate?' He held out a brimming tankard.

Midnight accepted it. 'No trouble, friend. None at all.' Still smiling he went with his new acquaintance to join the other seaman, asking if they knew Captain Daws.

He mentioned the incident in passing to Jess that evening, but she, overwhelmed by the rest of what he'd said, hardly took it in.

They were in the kitchen of the Hatchett which they had to themselves. Mat was down in the cellar bottling a new pipe of port, and Mrs Mat was lying on her bed nursing an aching head which she said was caused by an attack of the vapours, brought on more than likely by having to see to everything herself that day, while kitchen wenches went gallivanting.

But this carping was forgotten and even the strange visit to Jarman House slid into the background as Jess struggled to bring her thoughts together. She felt just as she had done the other night in the hayloft. Everything was on the move, flying away, taking off into the unknown and leaving her behind, as Midnight intended doing, except he was asking her to go along with him. She must look queer because he was asking:

'Are you feeling unwell?'

Yes and no was the answer to that. The queasy stomach had come back, hearing his idea, but she could hold steady to that, if only she could make sense of her thoughts.

'It is a beautiful country,' Midnight went on. 'Hills and valleys; the trees bright with birds of such colour they will dazzle your eyes. You would like to see them wouldn't you?' He was watching her anxiously. 'Is it the voyage that alarms you? A passage paid for is very different from working for your keep as I shall have to now I am one of the crew – though Captain Daws is an honest man with a good name for treating his men well. I care not how hard the work is so long as justice is observed.' As if to make her understand exactly, he took a small leather pouch from his pocket and opening it poured the contents on to the table. 'Fifty guineas, Jess. Enough to keep you in luxury the whole voyage.'

'No,' she said, stung into words at last. 'It ain't that I'm afeared of going to sea,' though it wasn't strictly true, she would be scared sick, 'it's after we gets there I fear.'

'What is there to fear? You won't be alone. We shall be together.' The words sounded false as he spoke them. He wondered what he was trying to do. Was his need of her so great? Or did he feel responsible for her – fighting off the terrible thought that this responsibility might tie him to Bristol.

Jess stared at him, trying to fathom both his thoughts and her own. But explanations kept slithering out of her grasp. All she knew was that, astonishingly, the whole of her was in revolt against leaving the place where she was born and bred. And that was the queerest thing of all, because she hadn't a home. Even the cupboard bedroom under the stairs where she slept was threatened. She'd known for a long time that once Mrs Mat saw her swollen belly she'd be sent packing. Now was the time to tell him, before it got to that. Now! Common sense said she'd need a man to protect and provide for her and the baby. One word and she'd keep him there. But that was as unthinkable as going to Africa. Oh why was loving so complicated? And when things got like this it didn't feel like love at all. She must try and give him a sensible answer. He was waiting. It turned out a question:

'Would thee've left thy home if th'hadn't been forced?'

He didn't answer for a long time. When he did it was with a shake of the head.

''Tis how I feel. If I went with thee I'd be nothing but a tiresome drab, wearing thee out by crying for home.'

'You might feel differently once you were there.' But he doubted his own words.

'I dunno. How can I know? And it be such a long, long way. What'ud I do then if I wanted to come home and there were no money and no ship to take me?'

'You paint a glowering picture.'

'Besides . . .' she began and hesitated.

'Besides what?'

'Oh . . . I dunno. I'm all of a muddle, it's come so quick. I ain't had time to think. It's best if we sleeps on it. The *Emerald* ain't going to sail for a while – three days was it th'said?'

'Three days – by the morning tide. And the Captain needs to know as soon as possible if there's to be a passenger.'

She got up. 'I'd best make a dish of tea for Mrs Mat afore she starts grumbling again.' She paused, then repeated: 'It's best if we sleeps on it,' coming close and putting her hand on his arm just for a second with a slight shake of her head before turning away.

He knew then what he'd always known, that there would come a time when they must part. That time was now. He sat stunned, watching her perform the menial task of making tea, reliving so many moments spent in her company; remembering the feel of her smooth skin, the scent of her, sweet and acrid, laughter they had shared and, more poignant, the vast gap they had spanned but failed to close. She would always be part of him and he would never forget her. Never!

Unable to stay there any longer, he got up and went out. It was the last time he saw her alone, and though they exchanged a few words on ordinary matters the next day, the voyage was never mentioned.

Before dawn two mornings later, Midnight bundled up his few belongings and left his room over the stable. In the yard he paused, looking hard at the back of the inn; grief strongly tempting him to wait and see her just one more. The temptation dwindled as rapidly as it had come, leaving only the grief – grief and a nudging breathless wonder because at long, long last he was going home. Goodbyes were anguish and he had no taste for them. Turning the five loose guinea coins in his pocket twice for luck, he left the yard and strode quietly and purposefully down to the river where, as the first pale fingers of sunlight reached out into the sky, he hired a boat to row him to the Kingroad.

Seventeen

Jess opened her eyes into the stuffy darkness of the cupboard bedroom. She yawned and stretched, then sat up because the lines of light poking in round the door told her it was morning. The regular sick feeling began and she sat still, breathing quiet and even – a trick to help herself that she'd discovered usually worked. It worked today and she began to dress, not hurrying, because she knew that being steady in her movements was the best medicine. It was a nuisance, this morning sickness, and she wondered how long she would have to put up with it.

Coming out into the ill-lit passage she could hear footsteps on the wooden floorboards overhead. Mrs Mat! Oh Lordy, she'd overslept. The fire should've been lit and the kettle on the boil by now. Forgetting all about being leisurely, Jess ran for the kitchen, arriving there just as Mat came through the back door, slamming it open with such violence that he dislodged a couple of saucepan lids from the shelf behind and sent them bouncing and clattering on to the stone flags.

Jess stared at him, mouth open, half expecting his temper to turn on her, but instead he went over to the table and flung something down. Midnight's pouch. It wasn't empty either! Her stomach lurched and she had to swallow twice before being able to ask:

'What's amiss?'

'Gone, that's what. Taken his bits and pieces and

211

vanished. This pouch bist all he left, and this . . .' He slapped a scrap of paper on the table beside the pouch.

Trembling with legs like lead, Jess picked up the paper. It was thin like Bible paper and had some bits of printing on it she couldn't read. Below were two words scratched in the brown of dried blood. She read her name as he'd taught her to – JESS. And out of the wild confusion of her racing thoughts a single inescapable realisation dawned. Midnight had chosen to leave a day early and now it was too late to tell him either about the baby or say anything about going with him. The thought swelled and swelled, dominating everything else. She heard Mat say:

'Where the bloody hell's he gone?' and saw the passage door open, and Mrs Mat come in; saw her take in the dead hearth, Mat's red face, ending up by staring at her and asking:

'What's going on here? Nothing's done. The fire's not been started . . .'

'Midnight's taken himself off. All he left were that pouch and a bit o' paper saying it were for her.' Mat jerked a thumb at Jess. 'Not a word for me or Mr Randall. What *he'll* have to say I hates to think!'

Mrs Mat opened the pouch and a little heap of guinea coins rolled on to the table. She looked at them greedily: 'Don't believe it! She knows more'n she's telling. Thick as thieves they were. Well then, miss, ain't th'going to say summat?'

What was there to say? Midnight had gone and there was an end to it. Stricken, Jess stared back. Mrs Mat took her by the shoulder and shook her. 'It ain't no use playing dumb.'

Jess felt herself heave. She said: 'Leave go of me!' and clapping her hand over her mouth rushed into the yard and was sick. Afterwards she leaned against the wall, limp and sweating, as Mrs Mat came out to scold and carry on about the fire not being made and having to do everything herself. The nagging voice was unbearable.

'I'll do it,' Jess snapped. 'Only give us a minute.'

'Th've had a few too many minutes, me lady.' Mrs Mat was looking up and down suspiciously. 'Been at the gin have thee?'

'No.'

'This ain't the first time th've been spewing. I reckon th'bist gone and got th'self caught!'

Jess didn't answer, but she couldn't stop the telltale colour flooding up her neck and into her cheeks.

'Th'little whore!' And it's that nigger as is the father. No wonder he's taken himself off.'

'That ain't the reason,' Jess said. 'He wanted to go home.'

'Home? He ain't got no home. Nor thee. I ain't keeping no nigger's moll in my house, so th'can clear up and go. And don't think as I'll be paying thee aught. Food and board th've had. That's enough.'

A spark of defiance broke through Jess's weariness. 'I wouldn't take th'money if th'begged me. I've enough of me own now.' She went back into the kitchen and scooping up the coins, returned them to the pouch. Mrs Mat followed her.

'Here . . . hold hard a minute . . .'

Mat caught his wife's arm as she put out her hand to take the pouch. 'It's hers by rights,' he said. 'Look on that scrap o' paper – "For Jess" it says. "For Jess" – he wrote it. And she's got troubles enough while we're provided for.'

Jess looked at him, surprised by this unexpected kindliness. It came to her briefly that he must be feeling a sort of loss as well. Different from hers, but just as real. Midnight was money to him, and pride for helping him be a better fighter. She tied the strings of the pouch with a brisk movement, feeling a burning in her throat and round her eyes. Other fighters would come along, but there was only one Midnight. Hurriedly she turned away, going to clear the ashes.

Within two hours she had left the inn. Mrs Mat had relented enough to give her a drink of tea and even offer food, but she'd been unable to eat anything. It was still early morning as she walked down the street. The money and pouch she had in her pocket under her skirt. A small reassuring weight but no salve for grief. Knowing he'd gone without so much as one word or a kiss was hard to bear and difficult to understand. But then there was so much about him she'd never understood. Where was he now? Perhaps he was still on the quay. Perhaps he hadn't found a boat to take him down river yet. Hope sprang up, bringing with it a great longing to see him just once more. She took a deep breath and told herself not to be so daft. It was over. By putting off deciding, she'd made the decision. There was no going back, and deep down she knew that it wouldn't have made a farthing's difference if he *had* stayed on till tomorrow. Her silent answer would have been the same.

So here she was, on her own again. Like old times, except she was better provided for. No! Not alone. Never alone again, at least not for months yet and perhaps not for years if she was lucky. She had the baby now. Midnight's baby, which was part of him to keep. And here she'd been slopping about in a muddle of thoughts that didn't do anything but make her feel worse, when what she ought to be doing was working out the best way of looking after them both. The money was a help and she was more than grateful for that, but they needed a home.

Blind and deaf to everything around her, she'd crossed

one street after another, scarcely knowing which direction she'd been taking. Now, as her spirits rose, she came alive to the city. Shops were trading. People leaned from upstairs windows, emptying slops, calling to one another, and from the top of the street an elderly horse and rider picked their way between the garbage. A cart rumbled past her and the driver called out a greeting. She waved to him, walking uphill, her feet going home without her head knowing.

At the tradesman's door of Jarman House, she paused. The old cow was hardly cold in her grave – perhaps she'd not be welcome? All the fragile confidence and hope that had been building up during her walk suddenly crumbled. Loneliness came back twice as real and a single dry convulsive sob escaped. Angry with herself, she refused to cry. With a shiver she opened the door and went inside, closing it with determination. Nobody ever got anything without a bit of cheek and grit.

She'd expected to go to the back door and was trying to steel herself against all the kitchen comment, when she heard the crunch of footsteps on the gravelled terrace screened by trees and shrubs. Looking between the leaves and branches she glimpsed a small familiar figure dressed entirely in black. To find Miss Phoebe in the garden at this early hour was so unexpected, her unreliable courage evaporated and it was all she could do not to run away. But the opportunity was so perfect she couldn't waste it and squeezing through the bushes, faced Miss Phoebe.

'I'm sorry to come on thee so sly, miss,' she said rapidly before panic set in, 'but I needs to talk to thee because I'm in that much trouble and . . . and . . . well, there ain't no one else as I can turn to.' Now that she'd got this far there was no retreat, but the last of her nerves deserted her. The plan seemed suddenly as full of holes as a sieve. She licked dry lips and her gaze slid away from the old woman, who had given a little jump of surprise and now stood puzzled and anxious, her hands clasped against her flat chest.

'How you startled me, Jess. Trouble you say? What kind of trouble?'

But Jess could find no more words. The upsets and turmoil of the morning overwhelmed her and she burst into tears.

Miss Phoebe said: 'Oh dear . . . oh dear me!' coming close enough to pat Jess's arm. 'Don't take on so. Please don't cry. Come into the house and you can sit down and take your time and tell me all.'

Still sobbing, Jess allowed herself to be led through the front door, thankful to miss any curious stares from Salt or Sally – shamed by her own weakness, but underneath grateful that the first obstacle was passed. She'd achieved a sympathetic ear. Now to test it!

Miss Phoebe took her into the morning-room and settled her into a chair by the window. With a great effort Jess swallowed her sobs, wiped her eyes and began to talk.

'*Expecting a child!*' Miss Phoebe said with a gasp when Jess had finished. 'I'm . . . well . . . that is . . .' for the time being words failed her. A faint pink flush suffused her face and she twisted her fingers together as if she would wring some sense out of them. She recovered enough to ask hesitantly: 'You did . . . er . . . love this young man I suppose? It wasn't just . . . er . . .'

'Yes I do,' Jess said, making it a living thing and hiding behind truculence because talking was so painful.

Miss Phoebe began twisting her fingers again, breathing as if she'd been hurrying, Jess shivered. She'd left nothing out, instinct warning her that hope lay only in complete honesty. But instinct could be wrong. In the ordeal of the following silence, she dared to glance at the old woman.

She seemed to have got over her first shock, but looked unusually grave. Her question: 'What do you propose to do now?' was asked in an equally serious manner.

No way of hedging this time. Tears wouldn't help again, thought they'd been genuine enough. Jess took a deep breath: 'Would th'let me serve thee, miss?' I ain't asking for wages, just board and keep,' beseeching with voice and look as intensely as she knew how, willing the old baggage to say yes. She had to wait a lifetime for any reply.

'You want me to take you in . . . care for you and the child? Do you *know* what you ask?'

'Yes,' Jess muttered, knowing all about the fingers that would point, the wagging tongues that gossip about old Miss Phoebe Jarman who'd gone off her head since her sister passed on and was keeping a servant wench as had gone to the bad; worse still, letting her bastard stay on in the house – a black bastard into the bargain!

'There's much to consider,' Miss Phoebe continued. 'Practically and morally. The servants . . . tradespeople . . .' She got up and walked about murmuring: 'God knows I don't wish to be unkind, but . . . impossible . . . impossible . . .'

As a last despairing throw Jess said: 'If th'could just see th'way to letting me stay on till the baby comes, miss, I'd be that grateful. After that we'll move on together . . . if she's spared.' Coldness crept into her marrow, but she wouldn't let her mind go wandering. It was now that mattered. She said defiantly: 'I'll take a chance on that. It ain't no different to the rest of living.'

'We're all in the Hands of God,' Miss Phoebe said. She stopped in front of Jess. 'I am sure He'll be merciful to us both.'

Jess looked directly at her and saw that the faded blue

eyes were moist. She didn't know much about God or his mercy, but she'd known enough of loneliness to recognise it in somebody else. She felt a touch of shame at not having given more than a passing thought to the old woman's grief. Her own problems shrank and she said gruffly:

'I didn't think too careful afore coming, miss. Th've troubles enough without taking on mine, I see that now.' She stood up meaning to go, but Miss Phoebe said:

'We both have been thinking only of ourselves. There's a child's life to consider.'

'She's likely to be black, miss,' Jess said, hardly daring to breathe.

'What better reason for persuading me, Jess. It seems like a sign. We talk and talk, but it's the doing that counts,' Miss Phoebe put out a thin tentative hand. Astonished, relieved and curiously moved, Jess took it.

*

The whitewashed attic bedroom was chilly, even though April sunshine streamed through the gabled window. Mrs Stocks pulled her shawl more closely round her shoulders and said:

'I could do with a fire . . . I feel that nipped.'

On the narrow bed, Jess felt another pain begin in the small of her back, growing round to meet at the front and spread down her legs. She sweated profusely, her breath coming shallow and rapid.

Mrs Stocks came across. 'Quickening up are they, me love? That's good. Hold on . . . that's it . . . that's it.'

The powerful sensation subsided, leaving Jess flopped out. She closed her eyes grateful for the brief respite, then opened them almost immediately as it came back again, stronger than ever, parting her bones, stretching out and round and down. Without knowing, she shouted as her muscles, taking on instructions that were none of her ordering, bore down with such force she thought her head would burst. Then they relaxed as the power died away and she heard Mrs Stocks say:

'Lovely. Oh now th'bist on the way. Thy baby'll be here afore there's time to make a pot o' tea.'

'Sooner I hopes,' Jess gasped. 'Were it like this for thee?'

'Eight times over, me love. And sweat . . . th'could've wrung me out like a dishcloth!' Mrs Stocks dabbed at Jess's forehead with a clean rag and nodded to Miss Phoebe who had opened the door a crack, enough to peer round without coming in. She mouthed: 'Is she all right?'

'Grand!' Mrs Stocks said.

Jess, her eyes shut again and the sweat coming, shouted: 'Oh Christ!' and Miss Phoebe, with one shocked look, disappeared.

In the shrinking spaces of peace between each push, Jess was vaguely aware that ordinary life was still going on. The sun danced across the ceiling and along the wall; birds sang; a dog barked; a door banged – but all this was outside time and her world, vanishing altogether as she was caught up in huge driving physical effort. Earlier, in the long gaps of waiting, she had thought a lot about Midnight, wondering if he'd ever reached Africa and feeling his loss more badly than she had done since the long-ago day she'd learned that he'd gone. Now there was no time for thought; no time for anything but gathering up her battered energy as each effort approached. She was too occupied to notice the regular visits, as first Salt, then Sally Dade, followed Miss Phoebe in quick succession.

'Keep going, lovie,' Mrs Stocks encouraged – and to

Sally: 'I'll be needing that hot water soon. Fetch it up and put another kettle on.'

Sally scuttled out and Jess grabbed at the thin mattress edges. 'Oh . . . Lord!' and then: 'Jesus save us . . .'as this time the power inside her didn't relent, strengthening into one last gargantuan push which she was sure would split her in two. But just at the moment which this was to happen, it was over, and total relief took its place.

'There you are, me love!' Mrs Stocks said, following that with: 'God preserve us, it's a real little nigger and no mistake!'

Jess said anxiously: 'Is she all right?' wanting desperately to hear a cry and not caring two straws for anything else.

Mrs Stocks chuckled, hooking her fingers round the baby's ankles. 'Finely . . . plump as a chicken,' She drew the baby up and Jess saw the thick ropy cord and heard a thin wail as the first breath was taken. 'But th'bist wrong on one count. Cept'n he's a bit overtoasted, he's as handsome a boy as anyone 'ud want.'

Jess didn't resent the remark. Too much joy pulsed through every artery and nerve, every muscle, every hair. Oh glory, glory . . . she'd done it!

She held out her arms. 'Give him to me,' amazed now that all along she'd expected a girl.

'Hold on, me lovie, we've to cut the cord yet.' Mrs Stocks laid the baby on the bed and rattled amongst the things set ready on a chest by the window, selecting a reel of stout linen thread and a pair of sharp scissors. 'A jiffy and we'll be done.'

'And what's his name to be?' Miss Phoebe asked much later when everything was tidy and Jess tucked up with the baby cradled in her arms.

'Jarman,' Jess said without hesitation. 'Jarman Olaudah,'

looking down at the perfect dusky skin of her son. Not Midnight black, but dark chocolate with a matching fuzz on the top of his small head.

Miss Phoebe was looking surprised but pleased. 'Jarman Olaudah Peters. That has quite a ring to it.'

'No,' Jess said firmly. 'Not Peters . . . Night.' It seemed appropriate.

'Jarman Olaudah Knight then,' Miss Phoebe said and smiled.

Under the weight of his name the baby's forehead rippled and puckered. His mouth pursed. A tiny fist struck out and he looked ready to cry.

'He knows what he wants all right,' Mrs Stocks said. 'A drinking man and he ain't after the port. Go on, lovie, don't mind us.'

Nervously Jess put the baby to her breast. After a false start he sucked vigorously and the strong tingling drawing sensation brought with it more love than she'd ever thought existed. Tears crowded her eyes.

'Hurt a bit, does it?' Mrs Stocks asked.

Jess shook her head. No words could tell what she felt. They were feelings – vast, burningly alive, and that was that. But one thing stood out granite hard and brighter than Samson's forge. Never . . . never . . . NEVER would she allow her son to be any kind of slave.

They could hang her first!

Author Biography

Marjorie Darke comes from Birmingham, she now lives in Somerset with her husband and enjoys music, gardening and patchwork. Marjorie embarked on her writing career, when she had children.

Her book A QUESTION OF COURAGE, about Suffragettes was shortlisted and highly commended for the Guardian Award and has been translated into many languages. THE FIRST OF MIDNIGHT was also a prize winning book and much translated.